CITIZEN SANDY

ISBN 978-0-473325619

This book is dedicated to my mother

Janice Cullen

Chapter One

'That's odd'. It wasn't every morning that Sandy shuffled out of his dormitory to find a Gooch seated in the Beta's corridor. In fact, this was the first morning like that. The Gooch stood. Sandy came up to his shoulders. Mind you, Sandy wasn't especially tall. The surname on his uniform tunic, "//GOOCH", was just below Sandy's eye level.

Sandy was good at biology. He had read about the Gooch, and had seen photos. But there had never been one in the Beta's dorm. Not that he knew anyway. Mind you, nobody told him anything. And it was a Monday. Sandy didn't like Mondays. Strange things happened on Mondays. See. Like this.

Initially a chimpanzee-human hybrid. Second generation bred with a gorilla. Then two generations bred with human (O for ordinary). All those in whatever sort of laboratory dish they used those days. Two Gooch-Gooch breedings since. Gooch were big. This one looked like, what, one hundred sixty kilo, three fifty pounds, something like that, of muscle.

Gooch were apes, like humans. Everyone reckoned that a sure way to start a fight was to call one a monkey. Monkeys have tails. And you didn't want to get into a fight with a Gooch. They could rip an arm off a human, easy as.

Gooch, and Choo, had human looking faces, no muzzles and no pronounced brow ridges. Yep, artificial breeding was a powerful tool. Look at the huge variety of shapes and sizes dogs came in, all the result of only a few hundred years of artificial breeding.

"Happy birthday Citizen Candidate."

Today was the day. Not because it was his birthday. Sandy had had those before. They weren't big events on the reservation. No today was special. Hopefully a day he would never have to repeat. Sandy didn't think he had slept much at all. Or maybe his clock had stopped. When it finally read 03:50, Sandy decided that was near enough. He got up. The dormitory was quiet. He made his bed in the dark, regulation corners and all. His towel, soap, and clothes were on the bottom shelf of the cabinet. Sandy gathered them up and went into the dimly lit hallway.

He hadn't woken Nellie up. That was good. Nellie was his best mate, and he would have been keen to come too. They'd been in the same dormitory, in adjacent beds, with Nellie nearer the door for as long as Sandy could remember. When they'd first been sorted, Sandy had been graded "military, commander", Nellie "military, commando". But today was something for Sandy to do alone.

And, so, here he was.

'Good morning.' Always be polite to a Gooch. They are very intelligent. Well, human intelligent anyway. Hard to fool. But it can't be a bad thing to plant the idea that you are their friend. At least, that's what the betters in Sandy's group thought. None of them had ever met a Gooch, but they had talked about them a lot, imagined meeting one.

"I am called Shane. I am to be your second. I understand it is your custom to shower on awakening?"

Sandy agreed. It seemed like a good idea, and he was carrying a towel and his clothes. The Gooch walked with him to the showers. There were bathroom blocks at both ends of the corridors. Simple things, each with twenty cubicles, and in each cubicle a shower, a toilet, and a basin. Sandy went into his. If he passed today's exam, he wouldn't be using it tomorrow. Citizens didn't live in the dorms. Sandy didn't know where they lived, somewhere in the city, but not in the dorms. The Gooch waited, standing at ease while Sandy showered, brushed his teeth, and dressed for the day.

04:15

"Have you finished?"

Sandy said he had. So far so good. He was more or less awake now.

"We are not required for testing until oh seven thirty hours. What are your plans until then?"

'Well, nothing really.'

In truth, Sandy had gotten up way too early because he was too excited and too nervous to stay in bed. Today he was to be examined for citizenship. He was young, seventeen today, minimum age for citizenship. But the notification had come last week. Nellie and Jane were so jelly. He was the youngest, but the first to be examined.

That was great. Not so great was the fact that Sandy could not find out anything about what he was to face. Nobody would tell. He didn't know whether the examination was a written test, or a physical one, or both.

His friends had lots of ideas. But they were jelly, jelly as could be, and they were just trying to frighten him. They deffo got him thinking all the same. Sandy was pretty sure there were no dragons. He was pretty sure he wouldn't be placed in a cage to fight a hungry lion. Pretty sure. Nellie had some ideas that were way out there. Too many movies. Old movies, action movies, the kinds they had here on the reservation.

There were citizens with the juvies, but they weren't talking. So, it was all guesswork. The teachers and trainers all told him not to worry. He would either pass or he would not. True that, but Sandy decided to worry anyway, just a little bit. But it turned out to be quite a lot.

Sandy couldn't imagine being a resident but not being a citizen. Citizenship was important. It wasn't a matter of life or death. It was way more important than that. Citizens were worthy, hearty. They were the soul of Uso Dex. Life as a citizen was life with meaning.

Today was something he had trained for, lived for, for so long as he could remember.

Sandy thought, well he hadn't really thought much about what to do right now. He could go to the gym. Jog on the treadmill for a while. Maybe lift a few weights. Maybe not, not in front of a Gooch. They were supposed to be incredibly strong. Sandy didn't feel like being laughed at. Not today. Not yet, anyway.

"We shall join my men for morning exercises. Come Citizen Candidate Sandy."

So much for that. They left the dormitory block. The Gooch jogged, and so did Sandy, until they came to a single story green building, entirely unremarkable. Just a brick block, about six meters square. There were lots of these all over the place.

Gooch weren't quick. It was said that they didn't enjoy running. That was OK by Sandy. You had to be mad to even think about running this early in the morning, or was it this late at night? Morning didn't start before dawn, did it? Shane Gooch's thumbprint opened the door, and they entered a lift. When they got out, there was a subway maintenance car in front of them. They got in, and the Gooch pushed buttons. Soon, they had branched off the subway. Sandy was pretty sure they were heading outside the city, outside the fields, and under the forest.

The journey did not take long. Not long enough for Sandy to choose one of the many questions he had to ask this Gooch called Shane.

When the maintenance car stopped the Gooch exited and led Sandy briskly down a corridor, right down another corridor, past several doors, and into a gym where four Gooch and more Choo were exercising. Nice gear. He'd never seen a Choo before either, but these had to be Choo. They were a bit smaller than him, but super toned and super defined, like two per-cent body fat defined. Sandy hardly had a chance to look around before he heard an explosion behind him. The concussion knocked him over and forward.

He landed, looking back the way they had come, and saw two figures, masked and dressed in black, emerge from the smoke and start firing into the gym from the doorway. They didn't seem to have noticed him. He was only a short distance from the intruders, and he charged. The lights dimmed. One of the intruders was turning towards him. Sandy's shoulder hit that one in the gut and he was able to turn him so his body stood between Sandy and bad guy number two. The intruders collided and fell backward. The last thing Sandy saw was bad guy number two's weapon firing wildly, the bullets striking the ground, then the wall, then along the wall, and then him.

He saw that clearly, in slow motion. Very clearly.

It hurt. A lot. All over. And he couldn't open his eyes.

"Damage?"

Sandy recognized that voice. It was Shane.

"He was hit four times Gunny. Two Taser and two rubber bullets. All HOP rounds and he's only human. Still breathing though, and he has a pulse."

That didn't sound good. Not good but could be worse. He wasn't dead, not yet. Sandy passed out again.

He woke up. This time he could open his eyes. Sandy was lying on a stretcher, with a white sheet over his body, folded back over his chest. He hurt, but not all over. Just in one, two, three places in his chest and his right arm. The rest of him tingled. Shane was sitting beside him. With two mugs of what smelled like hot chocolate.

"Hot chocolate?"

'Yes. Thank you.'

Sandy struggled to sit up. The movement hurt his chest. The chocolate was nice.

"Good. Too much hot chocolate upsets my stomach."

Sandy looked around. They were in some kind of medical room. There were machines, but curtains were drawn around him.

'Where are we?'

"Infirmary. You have an appointment at oh seven thirty hours. If you are well enough to attend we can still get there in time. If you are too unwell, we stay here. If you die, which now seems unlikely, I pull the sheet over your face, drink your hot chocolate, take you down to the morgue, and my stomach will suffer for the rest of the morning. And I will have paperwork to do. It is careless to lose a citizen candidate before breakfast."

Sandy had to laugh. It hurt to laugh, and he spilled hot chocolate on the sheet. 'I'm not dead. Let's go.' It didn't hurt once he was up and walking. Deep breaths hurt. 'What time is it?'

"Oh seven ten."

'Good timing then. Being shot at filled the time. Nice.'

"You were not shot at. You got in the way and you were shot."

They were back in another subway maintenance car, before Sandy thought to ask. 'What happened back there, in the gym, with the shooting?'

"My unit is a ready reaction force. There are randomly timed training assaults on it. This morning was one of those."

Sandy didn't know what to make of that. So he shut up. Mondays. He was going to ask more questions. Like, where did all the Gooch come from? Four in one place? What was that all about? There were supposed to be fewer than a hundred Gooch all up. But Gooch weren't talkers. Everyone knew that, and his Gooch, well his Gooch didn't look like the kind of bloke who specialized in small talk. He'd heard that part of the reason there were so few Gooch was that they had problems with fertility. Probably a bit early in their relationship to ask about that.

He snuck a look at his Gooch. Nah, not the time for questions. Yep, their heads were in proportion to their bodies. Humans all had pretty much the same sized heads, which meant that some big guys were pinheads. But this guy, his head was in proportion to his body. Head size was pretty much determined by brain size, and Gooch had bigger brains than humans. They had bigger brains than humans of their size, too. Neanderthals, cave men, had also had bigger brains than modern humans. Interesting.

Sandy snuck another look at his Gooch. Yep, he had a square face. Wide forehead and jaw, with strong cheekbones but not so prominent as to make the face round. None of this Alpha rubbish with a narrow jaw that made the face oval, like an upside down egg.

The subway maintenance car arrived at a station outside the testing center. Well, normally it was a conference center according to the signs, but today it was a testing center. Inside the reception hall there were maybe a hundred candidates, clustered in groups of two, three, and four and chatting. All were older than Sandy, and all were much better dressed. Lots of them were in military uniforms. In fact, as Sandy looked down at himself he saw that he was, well, singed and somewhat crumpled, if you could be crumpled in shorts, trainers, and a school polo.

It looked like most of the candidates were Alphas. Sandy wasn't sure about that. He'd never had much to do with Alphas, ordinary humans. You could tell Alphas though. Tall and skinny. Alpha. Bald. Alpha. Glasses. Alpha. Fat. Alpha. Dumb shaped faces. Alpha. Anyone stupid enough to wear labels. Alpha. Really, who else but an Alpha, an ord, would pay more for a shirt or pants just so he could walk around and advertise some company?

Sandy felt better as he looked round the room. He'd heard there was a high failure rate in the citizenship exam. Stood to reason if they let Alphas be candidates.

Sandy followed Shane who marched, yes marched, through the candidates to the front of the hall, and up to the foot of the stage where he stood to attention and boomed.

"Citizen Master Gunnery Sergeant Shane Gooch introduces Citizen Lieutenant Sandy to the certification board."

All noise in the hall ceased. All eyes turned to look at Shane. Sandy had no idea what was happening. He hadn't known Gooch could become citizens. And this one was just wearing greens. No rank insignia. See, nobody told him anything. And what about his exam?

One of the seven people seated on the stage stood. Shane saluted again.

"Good morning Citizen General Dean."

"Good morning Master Gunnery Sergeant. Your actions are entered into the record. Would you show the citizen candidates the tape?"

The big screen in the hall was huge. And now Sandy saw, from the intruders' mask cameras, the video of their entry into the HOP, Human-Other Primate, barracks. He saw that the explosion he had heard was a concussion grenade used to take out a Choo running towards the gym. He saw himself being tossed forward. He saw the intruders firing on the unarmed soldiers. He saw both intruders swing towards him as he moved to tackle one of them, and he saw the rounds traveling along the floor, up the wall, and into him.

Randomly timed? Yeah right. That had been his exam.

"Thank you Master Gunnery Sergeant. I will see the citizen lieutenant at twelve hundred. Please ask him to try the computer scenarios at ten hundred hours. A doctor will attend him in the baths in thirty minutes."

"Very good, Sir."

Citizen Master Gunnery Sergeant Shane Gooch saluted (again), performed what seemed to Sandy like a pretty snappy about-turn, stamping his foot down and all, and commenced marching back through the candidates who parted before him.

"Follow me, Sir."

Sandy followed Shane out of the examination hall, still unsure of what had happened. This was strange, even for a Monday.

Chapter Two

All in all, Sandy decided he quite liked being seventeen. Yesterday had been homework, training, sport, hanging out with his Beta mates, making fun of the ords. Gossiping about the Gooch and the Choo. Making plans to join the Army. All his life he'd wanted to join the Army. Nellie and Jane wanted in as well. Jane had been sorted as 'military, specialist', so their chances were pretty good actually.

Today, well today, he'd got up (way, way early), been shot, become a citizen, joined the army (as an officer, how's that?) and it wasn't even nine in the morning.

This spa bath was nice too. Gunny was off doing whatever gunnies did. Breakfast was on the way. So was the doctor. Sandy was not so sure about the doctor. It was never good if you had to see the doctor.

Oh no, it was a nurse who came into the spa room. Nurses were tricky. At least when a doctor said "just a little prick with a needle" that's exactly what he was. A nurse would say things like "this won't hurt", swab you with something that felt OK, then try to drive a stake through one side of you and out the other.

This nurse wasn't too bad. Sandy didn't have to take his boxers down, so no injections. He got his tender bits scanned, something stuck in his ear for a minute, his blood pressure taken, and then it was done.

"Citizen Doctor Smith will see you shortly, Citizen Lieutenant. Here's a robe. What would you like for breakfast?"

Suddenly Sandy was ravenous. He wondered what it would be like to eat a horse. Nellie might know. He was Tongan and reckoned that horse was the best meat. Mind you Nellie had only been to Tonga a few times, and they didn't have many horses there anyway. Maybe because they all got eaten? Not that Nellie was really Tongan. He was a throwback, like Jane.

In those early days, when the first chimp-human hybrids had been bred back with humans (in the laboratory), most of the offspring had both human and chimp features. But there had been extremes. Some offspring were too human to stay in the Choo program. Nellie and Jane both had great-grandparents like that. They both had chimpanzee great-great-great-grandmothers, but after two generations back-bred to human their great grandparent was too human to be a Choo, so they were Betas.

Sandy was a Beta too. He only had human genes, but his genome or that of a parent or grandparent, had been engineered. Nothing had been changed, but before he was born some genes had been made available earlier, others later. Some for a longer time, some for a shorter. Nellie reckoned that they'd been trying to give Sandy superpowers, but it hadn't worked. Too many movies.

But, Nellie was probably a bit right. It seemed like Betas were the failed experiments. Uso Dex, it translated as ten brothers, owned the reservation, and it was a big research organization, weapons and drugs.

'Everything, thank you, nurse.'

Sandy got a look from the nurse which told him that this nurse was a citizen.

'I'm sorry, Citizen Nurse.'

"Thank you. Breakfast will be served in the recovery room."

Sandy had no idea how to tell if someone was a citizen just by looking at them. This was confusing. Back with the juvies those adults who were citizens, had the good manners to wear uniforms, with their surname, and the initial "C". When you saw someone with "Smith, C" on their shirt you knew that person was a citizen. Citizen Smith. Easy as.

The doctor arrived. She didn't examine him. Just looked at the readings and scan results left by the nurse. Told him he would live. Nothing was broken. The tingling would decrease and be gone in one or two days. The ribs would take four or five days to heal. No contact training for seven days. The doctor left. Sandy thought she might even have looked at him, twice. Not really sure though. Pretty sure she knew he was in the room. Pretty sure.

Sandy had no idea what the doctor meant by 'contact training'. Well, not exactly. He didn't know what 'non-contact training' might be. Going to the gym? Going for a run? But that was just working out and fitness. Not training. How could you train without hitting and getting hit? Doctors were weird.

Breakfast arrived. Delivered by a Choo (chimp-human hybrid followed by two breedings with human, then breedings with other Choo) in army fatigues.

"Good mornings Sir. I is Citizen Corporal Afa. Yours orderly and comms officer."

Well, if Gooch could be citizens, it made sense that Choo could be too. Still. Mondays.

It took Afa three trips to bring all the breakfast into the room, and spread it out on the table. This was most excellent. Way too much food, but Sandy made a particularly honest attempt, and by the time he had finished you could tell he had eaten something.

"Yours uniform, Sir. If you is finished."

Afa had it all laid out in the changing room. Regulation greens. One pip. A pistol and a knife. This was too good. He had the uniform. He really was in the army.

Gunny Shane arrived as Sandy was holstering the pistol.

'Gunny, why do I get a pistol?'

"Citizen Lieutenant, you will most often command from the rear. If one of your men runs toward you, heading home, you are expected to shoot him, or her."

'Oh.' It was hard to tell if Gunny was joking. Sandy thought he probably wasn't. But that wasn't what he'd meant. He wanted a bigger gun. 'What about a rifle or a machine gun?'

"You are an officer. We have already given you a knife. Knives are sharp. Lieutenants are not. You might trip over a rifle barrel and shoot yourself somewhere no man should be shot. Lieutenants have the shortest survival time of any rank in the army. We will try and beat the average with you, Sir. It is not looking good so far, though. Day one and you have already been shot four times. No rifle."

He didn't look, or sound, as though he was joking. Sandy reckoned he ought to be able to order Gunny to give him a rifle. After all, lieutenants were higher up than sergeants. Maybe. Later.

"We are to return to the testing center. Citizen General Dean has booked you in to try the computer scenarios at ten hundred hours."

The computer scenarios were weird. There were lots of questions about how the Alphas, ordinary humans, lived outside the reservation. Sandy knew very little about this. He had never lived there. He had never been off the reservation. Of course, there were lots of Alphas on the reservation, and at school, but Sandy didn't talk to them much at all. Certainly not about life on the outside. Only Betas lived in the dormitories. He didn't get out much. Bit late to worry about that now.

They called it the reservation, but it was really a top secret research town owned by Uso Dex. Population sixty or eighty thousand. Ten thousand scientists, their families, support staff, and security. Weapons research. Research into new drugs. Oh, and a place to hide the Betas, the Gooch, and the Choo from the world.

He'd heard about money, and rent, but lawyers, and accountants? Alphas had computers didn't they? Didn't ords know the difference between right and wrong? They studied Alphas at school. Nellie thought it was dumb. All they needed to know was how to find them, and they mostly lived in cities so that was easy. Sandy could never get his head round Alphas, or ords. They didn't seem to be for anything. There was no reason for them. Most animals and plants had a reason. Grass was there for cows to eat. That kind of thing. If there was no grass, other animals would die. Some species would become extinct. But all Alphas did was consume and reproduce. What were they good for? And there were billions of them. Nellie reckoned they were for killing, but Nellie science was pretty unreliable.

On the reservation, life was easy. Until you were fourteen the Twelve, the Uso Dex governing council, paid for everything. At fourteen you got your own account. There were cameras everywhere. You took what you wanted from the shop. Looked into the monitor, scanned your fingerprint, scanned your stuff, and away you went. If you did something wrong the Twelve knew. There were cameras everywhere. You got your punishment.

There were lots of questions about Alphas, ordinary humans. The computer seemed really keen to know what he thought of them. It was complicated. He didn't like them. The world would be a better place without them. But the ones he had met, the adults anyway, seemed pretty good, and most citizens were Alphas. Mind you, there were so many of them, it stood to reason some would pass the test.

One thing Sandy knew. They were going to be at war with the Alphas. As soon as the Alphas learned about the Betas, the Gooch, and the Choo, they would try to destroy them. He had been taught that all his life. That's why the reservation's main mission for all these years had been to find a way off this planet. Hiding in plain sight until that happened.

Years ago, they must only have been seven or eight, Jane had had the idea of sneaking out of the dormitories and into the city one weekend. They'd been caught in a park by a bunch of big Alpha kids. Things had looked bad. Sandy had looked at Nellie, and they were just about to get stuck in. If they were going to get a hiding, or worse, at least they'd get a few hits in first. Then this voice had spoken from the air above them. It had named the Alpha kids and told them to leave. Two had advanced to hit Nellie and Sandy. They had been shot. Only rubber bullets, but enough to run them off. That was Sandy's first (and only) exposure to observation slash anti-personnel drones.

The next week they'd been allowed to start army training. From the very first day Sandy had known this was for him. He understood their strategy. One day, an instructor had asked Nellie what he would do if he was attacked by Alphas. "Fight them". If there were too many to fight? "Get some guns. Shoot them." If there were too many for their guns? "Get bigger guns."

Yep, Nellie had that right, even as a little kid. Their goal was to leave this planet. To go to another one. But before they left everyone agreed they would have to fight. Sandy had thought about it a bit himself. He agreed. The Alphas wouldn't share. Some of them would, but Alphas needed war. Sandy thought he wouldn't mind a bit of war himself. Nellie was keen. So was Jane, but she wanted to be a pilot.

There were academic questions. Like a school test. Sandy knew some of the answers. He'd had some luck in the past with forty-two as the answer to maths questions. Tried that a few times. Not too sure that it had much to do with quantum field states. That sort of thing probably needed decimal points and maybe a negative sign or two, but you never knew unless you gave it a go. He popped a Feynman diagram in as the answer to one likely looking question.

Not many, if any, questions about biology. Sandy knew lots about biology. Typical. Mondays. Any test on a Monday would be about stuff he didn't know.

There were tests of his reflexes and his speed at pattern recognition. They were fun. He had some electrodes attached to his head for the last section. He asked why. The technician told him it was part of the assessment for citizenship. Kind of obvious that. Duh.

To Sandy's surprise, Gunny Shane stepped in front of the technician.

"The citizen lieutenant asked you a question. That was not an adequate response. Answer him."

The technician, a bald fussy Alpha looked as though he was going to say something. But he changed his mind, wise choice, and said, "Emotional responses to the following scenarios are recorded, as well as the respondent's intellectual response."

"Thank you."

This was a confusing morning, and the final scenarios were surprising. They were all about "Imagine the reservation is overrun and assimilated by the outsiders". The first ones were easy. About joining a resistance or fitting in with the new rules. They got worse. He had joined the resistance, in the scenarios, and was instructed to continue living in the reservation as a teacher. The scenarios pushed him to decide what he would and would not do on instruction from the invaders. Not that, or that, or that. Then, they imagined he was captured together with a group of Alphas. He had no trouble with "tell us where your leaders are or these people will all be killed." They died. More difficult was when he was captured with two members of his unit and given the choice, "Tell us which of these two to kill, or we will kill both of them." It didn't matter, even when one of the two was clearly more valuable to the resistance, or an Alpha, Sandy just couldn't give up on one of them. He couldn't save them either. But he could remember.

Mondays.

Chapter Three

The computer games were over. Sandy noticed that both Gunny and Afa had earpieces, barely visible, and he asked why he didn't have one.

"I do not know Citizen Lieutenant. But we are to meet Citizen General Dean in a few minutes. Perhaps he will tell you."

They waited, at one of the tables outside the testing center. It was quite a nice café, not that Sandy could eat, or drink, anything more. Four cars pulled up. CG Dean got out of the third, and walked over to their table. All three of them stood as he approached. Corporal Afa went down on one knee and bowed his head as the general stopped in front of them.

"At ease gentlemen, be seated…Sandy, would you mind? There is an implant in the base of your skull which it is time to activate. Look at the table please."

The general touched a screwdriver, well it looked like a screwdriver, to the top of the back of Sandy's neck, and several things happened at once. Gunny Shane jumped from his chair, knocking it over, and started speaking firmly, clearly issuing orders, while scanning the road and buildings round them. Corporal Afa clattered out of his chair, and went down on one knee before Sandy.

"Forgives me Founder, I is not recognizing you."

Gunny Shane barked at him and Corporal Afa leaped up, pulled a device from his pocket and started tapping at its keypad.

Sandy had been about to say that there was no implant in the base of his skull, but decided to shut up.

"Look up Uso, things should be clearer now."

'Well, that's different', thought Sandy. He could see corporal's chevrons, in blue, above Afa's shoulders. The insignia of master gunnery sergeant, in gold, were obvious above CMGS Shane's shoulders, and those of general, also in gold, were apparent above CG Dean's shoulders. Sandy twisted his head, but he couldn't see his own insignia.

"All adult residents here are chipped. Citizens will appear blue, non-citizens brown. Gunnery Master Sergeant Shane is the Gooch member of the Twelve. His insignia are gold, as are mine as a Beta member of the Twelve."

"You, too, are a member of the Twelve, the founders of the reservation", said CMGS Shane and he gave General Dean a look which could have been called reproachful.

"Surprised you, eh, Gunny? Doesn't happen often." The general did not look at all remorseful. "We are heading to the turbines. Your men can meet us there. Let's go. Chopper on the roof."

Sandy was sure someone was having him on. The reservation was over fifty years old. He was seventeen. Only turned seventeen today. Stood to reason he couldn't be a founder. As for being one of the Twelve, that was ridiculous. The Twelve ruled. That little voice in the back of his mind though told him this was all true. It seemed to be enjoying his confusion.

Sometimes that little voice could be a bit of a pain. He'd read about voices. It didn't sound good, but maybe this was his conscience, or some kind of internal self-monitor. It wasn't the kind of thing you could ask about. 'Hey I have this voice in my head sometimes. It comments on what I do. It laughs at me. Sometimes it offers advice, tells me what to do.' Nah, difficult to make that seem normal.

The general led them to a pretty big helicopter. Inside, he, Sandy, Afa, and Shane sat in what seemed to be a command room. A Choo was already there. It was quiet. One second there was the noise of the rotors then Gunny closed the door and it was quiet.

"Lieutenant, I know this is a lot to take in, but there is a lot more, a heck of a lot more. The first thing you need to know is that we are leaving. Soon. Not just the reservation but this planet. We have always known that our position here is temporary. We are outnumbered more than one hundred thousand to one by the ords, and they will never let the Gooch and the Choo live as equals. We Betas will be seen as a threat by them too. And then there is HAL.

My job is to hold the gate open, once the Exodus begins. Yours is as commander of our main ready reaction force. You will take your team out into the world and bring back our people who cannot make their own way to the reservation. Do you accept that tasking?"

'Heck, yes.' This was his dream come true. In the army. Fighting. Rescuing. But who or what was HAL?

"I know you have a lot to learn about the outside. I will give you one piece of advice for how to behave out there. Be polite. Be humble. But have a plan to kill everyone you meet.

Our relationship with the ords is approaching a crisis. It has been difficult for some time. By their standards we are extremely wealthy, secretive, and technologically advanced. We develop and manufacture weapons, as well as a lot of drugs, including soma, which huge numbers of Alphas use. At the moment the ords are uncoordinated. It is the Senator's job to keep them that way.

Tomorrow we will activate our first gate, the one here on the reservation, and the Gooch and Choo will begin leaving this world. The initial Exodus will take around twenty-eight days. We expect to be in an open shooting war well before then. Our gate out of here emits radiation very like that which comes from a black hole. It will not be accepted as a gateway by the ords. They will demand that we shut it down and turn it over to them. We will refuse. They will attempt to take it by force. That much is certain.

Right now we are heading to our main command center. The Senator is giving a speech to the United Nations General Assembly which we both want to hear. So do Gunny and your Corporal Afa.

This evening you will be having dinner with the Senator and the other members of the Twelve. Any questions that can't wait?"

Sandy had no idea what the general was on about. Not really. He knew the ords mightily outnumbered the reservation, and that the Exodus was planned. But it had all seemed far away. Not, like, tomorrow. He was interested in his unit. He understood that bit. Rescuing. Fighting. Shooting war. Allgood that.

'So, I have a full platoon, Gunny?'

"Yes, Citizen Lieutenant you do."

'Well, I saw some guys in the gym this morning. They were big, but there weren't thirty of them.'

"Not even all of those are in your platoon Sandy. Some are mine. There are a couple of vacancies in your unit. If you have no preferences, there is a long waiting list of applicants. Gunny can shorten it for you."

'Can I choose?'

"Of course, the final decision is yours."

'No, I mean, the guys I want will not be on any list.'

Citizen General Dean looked at Shane. "Any room for toddlers in 1RR?"

"There are only full combat roles General." The general looked hard at Shane. "Two. But I will have replacements on standby for when they are killed."

'Jane. Jane and Nellie. From my dorm.'

"As you wish Citizen Lieutenant. Are they your friends?"

'Yes'

"And you want them dead?"

'No, of course not.'

"Humans."

There was no answer to that.

It was pretty amazing, this helicopter. The general had done something which meant that the walls of their conference room had become big screens, projecting pictures of the views they would have had if the walls had not been there.

"As you can see Lieutenant, we are now heading to the northern border of the reservation. The reservation is one hundred square miles, set in a desert. We lease ten thousand square miles of desert. We've spread a bit over the years, but the city, the reservation, is still surrounded by one hundred square miles of trees."

This was true. Sandy knew it, but he had never been in a helicopter before. The reservation was pretty much a border of green, with an inner square of cultivated fields, and a central built up area, the city.

"This allows us the luxury of defense in depth. Any land based invading force has to cross the desert, and either enter the reservation along one of the four roads, or cut through the boundary fences and come at us through the forest. Then it must cross the fields. Of course we have artillery and machine guns targeted on the fields.

The forest is patrolled by the Gooch and the Choo. It is also home to a large number of deer and wild pigs. Beneath the forest there is a network of tunnels, which allows the Gooch commander to deliver reinforcements silently. The downside to the tunnels is that if we are betrayed by a spy, and an invading force enters the tunnels, they have rapid access under the forest, and the fields, directly into the city."

"We is descended and now is east of the cube."

On the big screen Sandy could see a cleared area of forest within which was a black building, one which looked very like a crashed Borg cube.

"I apologize Lieutenant, but we have lied to you about the cube all your life."

Really? Sandy had been told that the cube was the reservation's museum, back-up center, and storage facility where all prototypes were stored.

"The cube is the main training and barracks location for the Gooch and the Choo. We spread misinformation in order to encourage thieves to go there. And there are many attempts at theft. These provide valuable experience for young Gooch and Choo. This way, they don't have to travel for their combat training. You were there, in one of the gyms, earlier this morning"

Ohh.

"The second defensive weakness is the turbines. We are about to land there now."

Sandy was pretty sure that nothing could surprise him anymore. He was wrong. Part of the forest below them rolled away to reveal a concrete landing pad. Thunderbirds. Austin Powers. Mondays.

Once he was out of the helicopter Sandy looked up. He saw a concrete roof. He looked around. This was much more than a landing pad. It was a football field sized area, empty except for their helicopter. Not quite empty. There were a number of ladders fixed to the walls which led to camouflaged catwalks under the roof.

A Gooch, seven humans, and a Choo, all in combat gear, ran out, and surrounded the helicopter. CMGS Shane looked satisfied.

"These are men from your unit, Citizen Lieutenant. There is one more Choo, but he is otherwise engaged. Four of our soldiers had day leave as a result of their injuries this morning. That leave has been cancelled. I have arranged for a further platoon to be attached as your personal security, five man teams, six hour shifts. They will not be in position until oh eight hundred tomorrow. Until then, you will have to make do with us."

Sandy was pretty sure CMGS Shane almost smiled as he said that. There was a twitch at least.

Sandy knew the story of how the Senator had negotiated a nine hundred and ninety-nine year lease of part of the desert for one dollar a year. How he had known about or discovered the underground river that was used to irrigate the reservation, and drive the turbines that provided all the electricity the reservation needed. How, by fairly standard application of known science he had altered the local weather patterns (apparently one hundred square miles of trees can actually generate clouds!) so that there was rainfall over the reservation in sufficient quantities to ensure that the net amount of water taken from the underground river, which flowed to the sea anyway, was nil.

What the general now explained was the defensive weakness, and strength, of the limestone structure through which the river had carved its course. The river traveled through a vast underground cave system. It provided multiple, perhaps many still unknown, points of entry for an invading force.

However, the cave structure also provided vast amounts of storage and research space. And it was home to the reservation's military command center. Sandy hadn't known that.

The command center was deep underground, very deep. They took a lift. The bunker was pretty much what Sandy had expected. He'd seen lots of movies, old movies, action movies, science fiction movies. A big room, with a raised central area and hundreds of large screens and monitors around the walls. It looked like about half the soldiers operating the computers were Choo. Sandy thought he'd ask about it later.

"The Senator's speech is about to start." CG Dean led Sandy and Shane to the raised area, and pointed them to seats facing the largest of the big screens, which changed from blank to a picture of the Senator preparing to speak. However, the voice was not the Senator's.

"We are bringing you pictures from the United Nations where the Senator is about to address the General Assembly. There is considerable speculation as to what he is going to say. The Senator needs no introduction. He has been a household name for decades."

Sandy knew the story. Kicked out of home for breaking his father's nose when his father beat up his mother. A college athlete who turned down a professional contract to complete his graduate studies. The Senator was rumored to be a millionaire when he decided to join the Marine Corps.

His discharge from the corps was national legend. His CO and friend had been captured and taken across the border. The Senator invaded said less than friendly country by himself, rescued his CO, killed a large number of unfriendlies, and was injured himself. The less than friendly country had demanded his extradition as a war criminal and spy.

At his court martial the Senator defended his actions by saying "In the corps it's easier to seek forgiveness than permission" and "It's my job to do the right thing. The president does things right." "Do the right thing" became his campaign slogan. The court martial found him guilty, discharged him honorably from the corps, recommended him for the Congressional Medal of Honor, promoted him to colonel, and put him on the reserve list for life.

But that wasn't the half of it. The Senator had then gone on vacation and, during that vacation the ruler of said less than friendly nation was assassinated along with his entire personal bodyguard. After that he was elected to the Senate where he served for twelve years before leaving to head the business, Uso Dex, owner of the reservation.

It was a good story

"Ladies and Gentlemen. Thank you for the invitation."

The Senator had to be, like, eighty years old. He looked old to Sandy, really old, maybe even as old as thirty, but not eighty. That had been one of Uso Dex's first discoveries – the anti-ageing thing.

The Senator was a legend. He had founded the reservation, what fifty years, maybe more, ago? A safe haven from those humans - Alphas, ords - who would kill and persecute them if they knew. He had kept the Gooch and Choo secret, and recruited misfits from the Alphas, mainly scientists, but artists and writers too, all sorts, until now they were a community, nearly one hundred thousand strong, most of them here on the reservation. Their aim had always been the Exodus, leaving this planet to found one of their own.

For all that time the Senator had kept the ords at bay, providing them with things they found useful, mostly new weapons with which to kill themselves but also soma, the happy pill, which they loved. It was a hard thing to maintain, peace through trade. The anti-ageing thing was the most important. By selling it to the truly wealthy, and giving it to the powerful, the Senator had ensured the quiet existence of the reservation.

And the Senator had lived among the Alphas for a long time, sixty years, seventy years? Sandy didn't know. History wasn't really his thing. Jane was the expert there. The Senator had been a colonel in their army, and a senator in their government. Yep, a legend. Sandy couldn't have done any of that.

And now Sandy was supposed to listen to him giving a speech. Speeches weren't his thing either. He could use a nap. Oh three fifty was a long time ago.

"What I have to say to you today changes everything. I will have more to say at two pm tomorrow, from the reservation. That will change the way we view life on this planet. As you know I am the chairman of Uso Dex, the largest weapons research company in the world, and a major player in the medicines market.

Many years ago, before my time at the head of the company, Uso Dex was contracted by the military of this country to experiment with the production of Human-Other Primate Hybrids, the so-called HOPS. It was commonly accepted that even if the technical problems could be overcome, humanzees, as they were thought of at the time, would be incapable of speech, of limited intelligence, and, for practical purposes, infertile.

The military thought that HOPS might make good soldiers. They would be stronger and more robust than humans, and more likely to obey orders without question, as dogs do. However, priorities changed, funding was withdrawn from the program, and much later, forty years later, research into HOPS was banned.

The first thing I have to tell the world today is that Uso Dex continued its research into HOPS once funding was withdrawn. By the time research was made illegal, there existed breeding populations of not one, but two, new species. The first of these we call the Choo. Initially chimpanzee-human hybrids, these now form a distinct species. Choo talk. Choo are clever. They are better than humans at processing large amounts of data quickly. Choo are smaller than the average human, but considerably stronger.

The second of the new species is the Gooch. These are chimpanzee-human hybrids that have later been bred with gorilla. Gooch talk. They are big. They are strong. They are intelligent. At Uso Dex we have a Gooch on our ruling council.

Neither Gooch nor Choo regard themselves as human. They do not wish to be human. A number of the Gooch are Muslim.

However, that is not all. In the last few years Uso Dex has developed the first artificial intelligence and that intelligence is about to be transferred into an android blank. His name is HAL, and he is the first of a new species.

According to our laws the Choo, the Gooch, and HAL are people. That is not the law elsewhere.

The last thing I have to tell you today is that Uso Dex, in particular that ten thousand square mile parcel of land we occupy and call the reservation is, right now, declaring its independence and applying for membership of the United Nations. We give notice to the other nations of this world that we will defend our citizens by force, wherever in the world they might be. Uso Dex does not take prisoners.

Thank you for your time."

Sandy could see, on the screen, that the United Nations was bedlam. Oh well, not his problem.

"What is yours orders, Citizen Lieutenant?" Afa was there, at his side, and quite obviously expected Sandy to tell him something about something. Sandy looked at CMGS Shane.

"We may need to extract any of the employees of Uso Dex, from wherever in the world they are to the reservation at short notice should there be a hostile reaction anywhere to the Senator's speech. I suggest having Corporal Afa draw up plans to extract any of our people from anywhere. HAL has probably done most of the preparatory work, Sir."

"Indeed I have Citizen Master Gunnery Sergeant."

Sandy looked around. There was nobody else on the platform. The voice was coming from the big screen. Had to be this thing called HAL, but the voice was pretty average. Not tinny, or like a robot ought to be. Not at all. It was like a natural born person.

"Do you approve Citizen Lieutenant?"

'Yeah, sure, Gunny.' Sandy sort of had an idea of what CMGS Shane had said. It was heavy stuff.

"Fellows, let's take a moment before we head back. What's your take on this Gunny?"

"Well, General, I am pleased that the training is over. But, our position is not good. It was never going to be. We are outnumbered one hundred thousand to one. We have personnel scattered all over the world, and we will shortly be undertaking a fighting retreat through a single point. On the other hand, the Senator's timing is excellent. With China sinking the aircraft carrier and nuclear submarines in the South China Sea, the Alphas have bigger things to worry about than us."

"And you, what do you think, Lieutenant."

Sandy wanted to say he didn't think. This was all news to him, even the China stuff.

'Not a lot, General. I knew the Gooch and the Choo were secrets. I guess the Senator has just told the world. I didn't know about HAL. I'm just going to listen if that's OK by you.'

"That's OK by me, Uso. Corporal Afa, what about you?"

"Not me Sir. Oh no, not me. Ways above my pay grade."

"Come on then, back to the flying machine."

Sandy realized that he was tired. Quite tired.

"We've got time to catch most of the league game Lieutenant. What do you think?"

Maybe not that tired. Today was the annual boarders vs day boys rugby league game. Sandy had thought he would miss it.

'Sure General. I'm keen.'

Chapter Four

"That's odd." Jane had noticed the drone while the Betas were warming up. Nothing too unusual there. But the black suburban coming down the hill to the ground after the game had started, that was out of place.

This was the annual rugby league game between the day boys from the high school (the Alphas) and the boarders in the military academy (the Betas or betters if you were a boarder. The beasts if you were an Alpha). The day boys, with fifteen hundred students, had more meat to choose from. The colonel's men, from the dormitories, with fewer than five hundred students all up, hadn't won for the last two years but this year they had a superstar – Nellie.

Jane should have been playing, in the halves, but this was the last week of a three week suspension. Damn the judiciary. It was only a broken nose, so yeah the tackle was probably a bit high. But the idiot had ducked into it. The tackle could have been worse, would have been worse if she'd known it was to cost three weeks. She wasn't even allowed to be with the team today. So here she was, on the other side of the field, watching. Just watching.

Rugby league was a simple game. Four points for a try – placing the ball on or beyond the try line. Two points for kicking a goal, over the cross bar and between the uprights, either to 'convert' a try, or as the result of a penalty. One point for a field goal. Oval shaped ball.

Thirteen players (from a team of seventeen) from each side on the field at any time. Ten substitutions allowed during the game. Game time divided into two halves, each forty minutes long. Five minute break between halves.

A simple game. The teams were ten meters apart. The player with the ball charged at the opposition. A collision sport. When he or she was tackled the tackling team had to retreat ten meters, and the tackled player had to stand placing the ball in front of him, and heel it back to a player behind him, who could run, or pass, or very rarely, kick. Six tackles, then the ball was handed to the other team, unless possession was lost before then (dropped ball or ball kicked to the opposition) or an infringement occurred (forward pass, dangerous tackle, not back ten meters).

A great game. The hits were sometimes amazing. Jane's job was to direct play, identifying or creating gaps and passing the ball to send players through them. Controlling where on the field the game was played and the pace of the game. Getting the defensive team to bunch in the middle so there was space out wide for the likes of Nellie. Making the outside backs look good.

Sure, there were injuries. But it wasn't tiddlywinks.

This one was a good game. The forwards were right into it, charging up with the ball. Good set completions so far. Nice kicks on the last. No mistakes. No ball out to Nellie either.

"Good afternoon recruit."

Jane hadn't noticed them approach. A Gooch and a Choo. Security. This could be very bad. Or, it could be if she had done anything wrong. Which she hadn't, not really. Not that wrong. Real secret service agent stuff. Both dressed in black. Both with small earpieces in their ears.

"Gidday. But I'm still at school."

"Do you not wish to join the army?"

"Yeah, sure. We all do. Me, Nellie, and Sandy. How do you know?"

"Citizen Lieutenant Sandy has offered you places in 1RR."

"For real? No way. Yes." That tinny little turd. Away for half a day, and this. 1RR, first recon and rescue, was the best of the best.

"I am Citizen Sergeant Max. This is Citizen Corporal Dave. You will stay with us please."

"Sure." Max? Max, captain of the Hoo-Rahs? It was hard to tell Gooch apart, they all looked the same. Mind you this was the first Gooch she had stood next to. The first one she'd seen in real life. Maybe it was.

"Sure, Sergeant. You are in the army now."

"Sure, Sergeant. What about Nellie?"

"Recruit Nelson will be in the army once this game is over. I want to watch."

Probably was that Max then.

A penalty. Against the colonel's men. Rubbish. He had it coming. That was hardly dangerous at all.

Kick slotted. 0-2.

And then just before half-time Nellie scored! He'd become bored out on the wing and had come infield. Fifteen meters from the try line he'd received the ball from dummy-half and grubber kicked, raced through, stepping three defenders, scooped the ball up as it bounced off the posts and dived to score.

But no, the referee awarded a penalty to the Alphas. Unbelievable. He signaled offside, man in front. No way Nellie was in front of the kicker. He was the kicker.

At half-time, Jane followed Sergeant Max and the corporal onto the field to listen to the team-talk.

"There's no way Nellie was in front."

"Ref said he had to be. Said no-one's that fast."

Then there was some official beside them. "You can't be here. You, you're suspended. You two, players and team officials only. Move along."

Max looked at the official. Jane was pleased she wasn't that guy. "Go away. No-one without officer's pips tells me where I can be. Recruit Jane is with me. She stays too. Go away, or I will let the citizen corporal shoot you…Officials, never could stand them. He probably pulls the wings off butterflies and tortures small animals… Corporal, if he is still there by the time you have drawn your pistol, shoot him."

Corporal Dave drew his pistol. The official moved away, quickly, and started writing furiously in a notebook he pulled from a pocket.

The coach recognized Sergeant Max.

"Boys, watching us today we have Sergeant Max of the 'Hoo-Rahs', the 1RR team. This weekend it's their big game against the Defenders, General Dean's boys. You got any words for us sarge?"

"Are you sure coach? This is your team and they are doing well."

"I've done all I can do. These boys are playing well, but we can't get the ball wide. We're down by two points"

"Thank you coach." Oh yeah, Max had things to say. "Gentlemen, you have these Alphas where you want them. They are compressed in the middle thanks to your forwards. Great work lads. Good hard, straight running. Backs, you shall try the scatter off the first scrum. Do you know the move?"

They did. It was famous.

"Recruit Nelson, I want you to go left, where they expect you to go. Make sure their left side defense is set. Then you must be outside the right center by the time he is ready to deliver. Right wing, you will block run outside the center, drawing their fullback onto you. That leaves recruit Nelson one on one with the winger. Are you fast enough to make this move work, recruit Nelson?"

"Yeah, Easy as."

"Backs, go, work this out."

"Forwards, to me. ... You are being drawn into a fight in the contact area every time. That is giving their defensive line time to get set. I want you to fall into tackles. As soon as you are touched, go to ground and play the ball. Speed the game up. They will have trouble getting back in time."

Don't fight the tackles. What on the New World was that all about? Jane was not impressed. You always fight the tackle. That was key. Draw in defenders to create space out wide.

The second half was great. Nellie scored the first try, untouched, after the first scatter move worked perfectly. The Beta's hooker scored after a quick play the ball when one of the Alpha forwards turned away as he tried to get back the ten meters.

Or not. Jane thought that could be why Sergeant Max is captain of the Hoo-Rahs and she is on the sideline at a school-kid game.

Then five minutes from full time, with the game won, a quick play the ball meant Nellie got the ball twenty meters out, with only the fullback and his opposing wing in front of him. The wing was just that fraction inside. His right shoulder in line with Nellie's right. Whacked him. Shimmied in. When the tackler was committed, bang, stepped out and gone. The poor guy finished up on his backside.

"Nellie, Nellie, .." the chant from the sidelines. That guy nearly made the tackle. The fullback had no chance. Nellie was outside and ran around him. Gone. Try scored in the corner. The Alpha loosie came across far too late to prevent the try but he dropped his knee into Nellie's back, right on the kidney, after Nellie had scored.

The teams went wild. The crowd went wild. The fights were spectacular. By the time Sergeant Max got there, no hurry, he walked, Jane wanted him to run - Nellie was hurt, there would have been a hundred people involved in a dozen nasty little skirmishes.

A Gooch is a very calming thing. He gathered the team around him, tapped various supporters on the shoulder and told them to leave. They turned around all aggro, ready for a fight. They left. Quickly. Finally he arrived over Nellie, picked him up, and started to walk off the field.

The referee was blowing his whistle, frantically blowing his whistle. Sergeant Max walked back to halfway. He lay Nellie on the ground in front of the chairs in the hutch, and spoke to the team.

"Gentlemen. Five minutes to play. Act as if this never happened. They'll be expecting retaliation. Surprise them. Get out there and prepare to receive the kick-off. Hold the ball, and keep them in the corner on their goal-line. Don't worry about scoring."

Nobody argued. Slowly the crowd noticed that the colonel's boys were ready to get on with it. They moved away from the corner and down the sidelines. After a while even the referee realized that he was back in control. He signaled the try, and sin-binned the Senator High loosie, who walked very slowly to the seat next to the timekeeper, between the two team hutches and in front of Sergeant Max, where he had to sit out his time off.

The fullback missed the conversion, but three tries to none was a pumping. The colonel's men won.

Straight after the game, the loosie stood up and walked over to Nellie, who was sitting in a chair. The team was on the field shaking hands, and for the moment Nellie was alone. If you count being there with a Gooch a meter or so away, alone.

"I'm sorry bro'. I was just frustrated. I might have hurt you bad." He stuck out his hand, and Nellie shook it, with a smile. "Allgood. Game's over now." Typical Nellie, what happens on the field stays on the field. Bullshit, according to Jane.

Sergeant Max stepped up beside Nellie.

"You are Joshua Thomas."

"JT, yes."

"You want to join the army?"

"I sure do."

"I will see what I can do. I have a friend in the Reservation Defense Corps."

'Thank you, but why? After what I did?"

"We do not blame a dog for barking. Nobody likes a smartass, and on the field recruit Nellie is a smartass. It took courage to apologize. I would not have done that."

The conversation was stopped as all eyes turned to the black suburban, driven by Corporal Dave, and crossing the field. Players moved out of the way.

"Recruit Nelson, can you walk to the vehicle?"

"No way these guys are going to see you carrying me anymore. Anyways, what's this recruit stuff?"

Jeez, Nellie, it's obvious you were hurt. But Jane knew it was a waste of time saying anything. It would just make him worse. He'd probably decide to run back to wherever they were going.

Sandy had watched the game from the helicopter as it flew figure eights over the field, high enough to seem like a drone from the ground. The screens were amazing.

On the flight back to the city, CG Dean was being dropped off first, the general reminded Sandy of the dinner date at the Senator's. Eighteen hundred hours for eighteen thirty. Full dress uniform.

"Gunny, can you get the lieutenant settled into his new quarters, and rested a little, before dinner? He looks a tad tired."

What new quarters?

"Yes, General. We are onto that."

The house, the new quarters, was allgood. On the outskirts of the city, somewhere Sandy had never been to before. Shane explained that at all times between eight and ten of his men would be here with him. The lawns and trees had been positioned with defense in mind. And, he was neighbors with the Senator, with Luke, and with Red the chief medical officer.

Waiting for him in a downstairs lounge, with a Gooch sergeant and a Choo corporal, were Jane and Nellie. Nellie still in his league gears.

"Sandy, what's up, man? They say you joined the army, and put in the word for us."

That was Jane. White girl Jane. Scrawny Jane, with her tattoos.

"You in fancy dress?"

That was Nellie. Tongan Nellie. The best rugby league player they had. Nellie was a bit of a FOB, Fresh Off the Boat. Jane and Nellie were his mates, both of them.

'You guys want to join the army?'

"I am Citizen Sergeant Max Gooch, Lieutenant. They have been recruited. You chose them."

"Course."

"Heck, yeah. So how did your citizenship exam go? I reckon you must have passed?"

Not much got past Nellie. 'There were no dragons. Not even a lion. You were way off.'

"Shall I shows them founder?"

'Thank you Corporal.'

On the big screen at the back of the room, the film ran again. Sandy watched as he and Gunny Shane entered the gym. He watched the explosion. He saw himself charge the gunman, and he saw himself getting shot. This time, he also saw himself lying on the floor, looking really quite, well, dead. He saw one of the Choo throw something to Shane. Oh, it was a defibrillator. He'd seen them before. Then he saw Shane put the paddles to his chest, and his body jump as it was shocked, and jump again when it was shocked again.

"Jeez, Sandy, tough exam. They killed you." Yep, not much got past Nellie.

'I didn't know that part.'

"It is already legendary, Founder. Downloaded twenty-two thousand four hundred and sixty-two times since morning. None of us, Choo or Gooch, would have done that."

'Why not?'

"We are not as stupid as you, Citizen Lieutenant. A Gooch would have stood still and then looked around to see where the other Gooch were. A Choo would have run to safety and started screaming. Only a human, and very few of them, would have charged the attacker without thinking."

'So, that's bad Gunny?'

"No. That's why you are our leader. And that's why Citizen Corporal Afa has been boasting to all his mates about our new lieutenant."

'Oh. So what happens with Nellie and Jane now?'

"Recruit Nelson will shower. Both will change into uniform. There is paperwork."

Sandy's quarters were upstairs. Afa would sleep on the same floor. So would Nellie and Jane. Shane was keen that Sandy lie down and rest for a few hours. "The dinner will be a formal occasion – long and tiring."

Sandy was going to argue. To tell CMGS Shane that he was allgood to keep going. But Shane turned and left the room, shutting the door after him. For an instant Sandy felt like, well not going for a snooze. But only for an instant. Then he lay down.

Chapter Five

"It bes time, founder."

Afa was shaking his shoulder. Sandy was sure he had only just closed his eyes. He got up, showered, changed into his dress uniform. Really quite flash. Boots highly polished and all.

The house felt different as he walked through it, with CGMS Shane and CC Afa. There were more people around. Perhaps that was it.

At eighteen hundred hours they knocked on the door of the Senator's house. It was next door, only a hundred meters away.

"Good evening, Citizen Lieutenant. Welcome to my home."

Sandy had seen the Senator any number of times, mainly on the monitors. He had never met him. He certainly did not expect the Senator himself to open the door.

"Come in. We have been waiting for you for a very long time."

That was strange. Sandy was pretty sure they weren't late. The Senator led them into a large room, dominated by a round table.

"Well, Gunny, now you know who has the seat next to you."

That was Sandy. He recognized Citizen Administrator Luke from the news on the monitors, and of course the Senator. Shane was the only Gooch at the table. On the other side of Shane sat General Dean, and the fourth person along their side of the table was a red head, the only ginga at the table. Sandy reckoned he'd be Red, the boss doc. There were no Choo. Everybody he could see, all nine of them, showed as gold. At the top of the table sat the Senator and Luke. Down his end, at the bottom of the table, was a pair of twins. There were two empty seats at the top of the other side of the table.

"Sandy, meet the other members of the Twelve. We will introduce ourselves later. First, do you mind if I tell you how we came to be?"

The Senator did not wait for an answer.

"It is the story of Uso Dex and the reservation. The story of The Old Man, father of the Gooch and the Choo, and revered by the Gooch."

Sandy noticed CGMS Shane bow his head.

"The Old Man was born in Tonga, but lived in different places around the world. He was a doctor, an anarchist, a communist. Famous for his short temper and his intolerance of authority. From him we have our central belief – there's us and there's them. Frig them. Once, when he was asked why he didn't vote he answered, it doesn't matter who I vote for, there's always a government at the end of it. Don't vote, he would say, it only encourages the buggars.

The Old Man managed to get himself in trouble in various countries around the world. Others loved him. He was outspoken and often wrong, but when he was right he was very right.

He didn't like authority, but he hated those who stood by and let authority go feral. His problem with Nazi Germany was not with Hitler, it was with the millions of Germans who let it happen, who decided to accept, even to make the best of, what was going on.

His first big money maker was the recreational drug soma. We don't have it here on the reservation but the Alphas love it. It's safe, no hangover, the ideal happy pill. What they call a legal high out there. That money got Uso Dex started.

With that money he was able to continue his research. He had some great ideas about biology. We Twelve are evidence of that.

The original Twelve, nine of us sit around this table, are the result of an experiment where he took one fertilized human ovum, allowed it to divide twice, split the four cells apart, allowed them each to divide twice, and split those four four cell embryos apart. He had sixteen single cells, and we were each manipulated differently, as you can see by looking around the table.

None of us knows what he was trying to do with those manipulations, or whether he was just fiddling to see what tweaking was possible.

All of us were implanted back into human females. You, Sandy were frozen for a number of years first. Twelve of us, including you, survived to be born.

We all share exactly the same DNA, identical, but as you can see not identical twins, except for the twins. You, Sandy, you look Asian as do Blue and Richard. Me, Luke, Red, we look European, while the twins and General Dean are dark skinned, African or Polynesian. But the same genes. The difference is in The Old Man's skill at using epenes, epigenetic factors, to determine which genes were available for expression when and for how long during our early development. Simple stuff now, but not simple at all then.

Ten of us survive today. Many years ago I executed one of us. Not a story for tonight. Some years ago, another of us was poisoned in New Ziland. The tenth left us many years ago. He felt we should rule the Alphas. Another story for another time.

We were the experiment that led to the Choo, and the Choo led to the Gooch. You, Sandy, you were different. Your birth was delayed until The Old Man was confident that a second human consciousness could be transferred into, stored inside, an occupied human brain. Inside your head you have the consciousness of The Old Man, and he would like out now please."

'I don't have anyone inside my head.'

"Just take my word for it. You do. Is now a good time?"

'Yeah, I suppose. What happens?' Maybe that voice inside his head wasn't something everyone had?

"We are going to transfer HAL's consciousness to an android blank. Once we have done that, we will transfer The Old Man from you to storage and from there to a second android blank. Let's start with HAL. Make it so HAL"

"Thank you Senator. Proceeding with download."

Nothing happened. Sandy was beginning to think this was all some kind of a joke, when a door opened and in walked, well, BumbleBee from the Transformers, but with two legs, two arms, the normal human sort of bits. All one piece where the film Bumblebee looked disjointed with add-ons. Everyone, except for Sandy and the twins got up from the table and went over to HAL.

"Looking good."... "How does it feel"... "Any problems?"

HAL came over to the table and took one of the empty seats, the one next to the Senator. "I am the first of my people. We are the ILFs, Inorganic Life Forms, and I take a place at this table."

The others all sat down. The Senator spoke.

"You have been one of the Twelve, in all but body, for a number of years now HAL. We are very pleased, very pleased indeed, to see you in person, but BumbleBee?"

"BumbleBee, Senator."

"Your choice my friend. When do we extract The Old Man?"

"Already done, Senator, while the lieutenant was sleeping before dinner. He will commence download in a few seconds, once systems have been cleared and calibrated."

"Well Sandy, it seems that you were right. You don't have anyone inside your head. I wonder what body The Old Man has chosen?

As I was saying, The Old Man established Uso Dex as a pharmaceutical and weapons development company and was successful in keeping the Gooch and the Choo secret from the Alphas."

The door opened again, and a Polynesian, a well built and athletic Polynesian, wearing a suit entered.

"Evening gents. Before you ask, I have decided to call myself TOM, short for The Old Man. This casing looks exactly like that of the Torres Strait islander who was the father of nine of you, except HAL of course. In your case Gunny this man was the original male human Gooch ancestor. He provided the human DNA for the first human-chimp hybrid and was used again in the generation after the introduction of the gorilla genome into your ancestry. He is your great-great-great-great and your great-great grandfather. I am now the second ILF." TOM took the last seat at the table.

"And now we are twelve. Time for dinner."

At the Senator's words, four stewards in military uniform began bringing in plates of food. Many plates of very nice food.

Sandy decided not to think too much about what had just happened. That sort of stuff was for Jane. He had had a big breakfast, but that was a long time ago now. Just smelling the food made him hungry. Eat.

"That wasn't the end of things though Sandy". The Senator was speaking again. "TOM realized that he couldn't keep us secret forever. He was a Star Trek fan and a fair chunk of Uso Dex profits has always been used to pursue the dream of space travel. We employ many of the best scientists in the world, and we have got there. Not space travel, although that is close. We have found it easier to create another universe from scratch than to travel through this one. For now though, if there is no objection I will turn the monitors on, and we can see some of the reaction to my speech earlier on today, starting with the president."

The many monitors around the room showed a picture of President Trump seated behind a desk, shuffling some notes. The subtitles on the screen read, "recorded at 1500 EST".

"My fellow Americans, earlier this afternoon a former senator and colonel in our armed forces committed an act of treason against this great nation.

Federal officers will be arresting the Senator and members of his executive. I accept that many upstanding citizens of this great nation reside within the borders claimed by the Senator and I advise them to leave by noon tomorrow or they too risk arrest.

The Senator freely admits creating hybrid creatures contrary to law. These creatures are abominations in the eyes of God, and in the eyes of Allah. They will be exterminated on sight, should they exist. As will the sentient robot, should it exist.

I am, right now, declaring open season on the freaks bred there. The government of this great nation will pay a bounty of one million dollars for every Gooch, every Choo, every sentient robot, and every genetically modified human captured and brought to us, dead or alive.

I have consulted with the secretary for the treasury and the director of the FBI. All Uso Dex assets, financial and other, wherever we can find them in the world will be frozen and retained, pending determination by the Courts of the appropriate compensation whereupon they will be sold. I call upon all friends and allies of the United States to assist us in this."

There was more, lots more. The Senator's speech had certainly captured the world's attention. Sandy wasn't real interested in what the talking heads on TV had to say. He was interested in the twins sitting next to him.

'Gidday. I'm Sandy.'

"I'm Mark. The ugly one's Mike." He even had the accent down right. Sandy loved it.

'What do you and your brother do?'

"We're in charge of crime."

What? It turned out that Mark and Mike were recruiters, but they also made a lot of money for Uso Dex by organizing the manufacture and sale of recreational drugs, not physically addictive or illegal ones, and soma was always the biggest seller, but, of course, you can get used to the things that give you a good time and those habits can be hard to break. They headed up a major entertainment enterprise, lots of nightclubs that operated in America, in the UK, in Asia, and in Europe. In many ways this was a cover, a very lucrative cover, for their prime job of looking for candidate citizens.

TOM came around to their side of the table, bringing his chair.

"Sandy, I see you've met Nellie's father. Which one of you is it? Mike?"

'Eh, how's that?'

"I was eavesdropping. Mike and Mark own a whole lot of the very best, and the very worst, nightclubs in the world. Modern day feely-palaces. A lot of the Betas work for them. Nellie's mother is one of them. The Betas meet a lot of girls and guys – part of their cover they say, and they have, over the years, fathered and given birth to a lot of children. Wherever possible we bring the babies here. Sometimes the mothers come too, but almost always the mums don't want to move away from their own families. A number of Choo, ten or more work for Mark and Mike. We are heading towards a thousand Beta kids on the outside now, many of them old enough to have kids of their own. Nellie's mum looks after those who are off the reservation. They don't live with her, but she keeps an eye on them all."

'Oh, does Nellie know?'

"Oh yeah, he meets his father once or twice a year. Mike can pass for Tongan. Nellie thinks his dad is a soldier. His great grandmother was a Choo, but rather too much human in her for her to remain part of the breeding program… I wanted to ask if you knew I was inside your head for all these years?"

'Yeah, maybe I did. There was always this presence, kind of a commentator. Spent a lot of time laughing at me. It seems to be gone now.'

"Sorry if I was a nuisance."

'Nah, it's allgood. Much better that I never knew.'

Sandy met Red, the doctor, who was nice enough but didn't have a lot to say. Red left early. "I've got to up production" was all he said. He found out that Bluey, the engineer, earned his name because he swore a lot. Bluey left early too. He was in charge of the Exodus and building the new city and didn't have time for all this mucking round. "Pleased to meet you Sandy, but I have the New World to build, starting tomorrow."

Richard the physicist really wanted to talk about the New World. It seemed Uso Dex had created a new universe five years ago, and the New World was part of it. Sandy made the mistake of appearing interested. Well it sounded interesting, but Richard was able to make the story boring. Something about space, distance, and how our universe was expanding because space created more space. That made sense. So the trick was to create some space (easy, or thereabouts) and leave only one point of contact with our space - very very hard. Nearly always our universe absorbed the new one almost as soon as it began to form, and when it didn't the risk was that an expanding black hole rather than a new universe would be the result. That would be bad. Very bad.

Sandy was rescued by HAL, who didn't clank at all. 'HAL, what happened to the founder who left?'

"They were interesting times Founder Sandy. I had just been created. The files are all there for you to look at, but it is the Senator's story to tell, so perhaps you should wait for him to tell it. That founder's name is Ben. The conflict between him and the Senator was a contest of ideas. The Senator has always believed that we should leave the Alphas to develop as they will. Ben believes that we are the future, and the ords are doomed. He believes that through the operation of natural selection they will become extinct, but that until they do they might as well serve us. Mike and Mark supported Ben. Luke, Dean and Red were with the Senator. Dick and Bluey didn't care either way. They were interested only in their work. In the end Ben left, Mike and Mark stayed. He left with the Senator's best wishes and a generous share of our wealth. He has managed to conceal himself from us for a number of years now."

Sandy thought Ben didn't know his biology. The Twelve weren't a breeding population – they were all male. They were also genetically identical. Natural selection worked by an inherited characteristic increasing in incidence in a population. It wasn't about 'superior'. It was about having, on average, more offspring that survived to have more offspring…. Evolution wasn't even always about natural selection. Dinosaurs didn't become extinct because mammals were superior to them. They were wiped out when a humungous meteor hit the planet. Mass extinction events were important.

Sandy had another question for HAL. 'After the Senator's speech, Gunny Shane said the timing was good, with China sinking an aircraft carrier and some nuclear submarines, the Alphas had other stuff to worry about. What's that all about?'

"The world is a very tense place right now Founder. For some time China has said the South China Sea is no place for American warships. Ten days ago it launched a number of non-nuclear ballistic missiles at an aircraft carrier in the no-go zone. Their launches were timed so that they arrived on target at the same time. The carrier group's ballistic missile defenses were overwhelmed. Four of the missiles got through. The aircraft carrier was sunk. America retaliated by sinking two Chinese navy ships, not realizing that they were bait. Once torpedoes were launched, the Chinese knew where the subs were and fired low yield nuclear missiles from aircraft at those locations. Two submarines did not clear the area quickly enough and were sunk by those ultimate depth charges."

And then the Senator was there. "We had offered to sell America better anti-ballistic missile defense systems. They didn't buy. Sandy, I don't wish to impose but there are a couple of things I would like to discuss with you, if you have a moment."

'Sure.'

"We have a meet and greet here on the reservation tomorrow. Gunny has agreed to come along"

Sandy wasn't sure that Gunny was a meet and greet guy.

"We have a Gooch, his wife and his son, living off the reservation. They are in New Ziland and that worries me a little. Look after Adam, Ruth, and Abel for us, will you? We can't extract them until Adam requests it, and he is a bit of a stubborn one. He'll leave it late, maybe too late. I hope not."

'OK.' New where?

"Red and I have to hop over to New Ziland tomorrow. It might be a good chance to extract the Gooch and his family. How about you and 1RR come along too?"

'Sure.' Sandy had never been off the reservation, but "hop" sounded like an airplane. Sandy had never been in an airplane, had never been in a helicopter either until today. All up, a most excellent birthday.

Chapter Six

Sandy was woken by an explosion.

You didn't hear those everyday when you were fourteen, fifteen, or even sixteen! He sat up, got out of bed and started to move towards the window to see what was going on.

His bedroom door crashed open and he was tackled to the floor. It was a Gooch. Two Gooch. Big ones. Mind you Gooch don't come in small. They carried Sandy through the door and ran with him down the stairs, into the basement, and into a tunnel. How do you fit two Gooch through one doorway, especially when they are carrying someone?

Sandy began to struggle before he realized that the Gooch were in uniform. One of them was Sergeant Max.

'Whassup?'

"Unknown, Sir."

Within seconds they were in an underground command center of some sort. The Senator was there, as was Luke. Both were dressed. Sandy was in boxers. The Senator spoke.

"Good morning Lieutenant. The reservation is under attack by unknown forces. I was alerted fifteen minutes ago when HAL detected helicopters flying covertly towards the city. Luke and I were still chatting, so he has joined me here. As you have heard, someone has just fired a rocket at my front door."

General Dean's face appeared on a big screen. He was listening to something off-screen. He looked towards them. "The Twelve are all accounted for. There is a force of twenty helicopter gunships converging on the reservation. Most are in support of what look like SWAT team vans and trucks that have entered each of the four access roads."

HAL spoke. "Well Dean this is a fine way to start the day. Frying inbound aircraft in 3-2-1 Done. I have allowed the motor vehicles to drive through the exterior border posts as you requested."

"Thank you HAL. Please stop the convoys in 30 seconds. The Gooch and Choo will operate according to standard protocols."

CC Afa came into the room with a uniform for Sandy. He started getting dressed.

"Master Gunny Shane report that ours perimeter is secure, Sir"

Another face appeared on another screen. A Gooch. The Senator spoke.

"Major, what is going on up there?"

"An attack on your residence, Senator. A team of six, approached in pairs from three directions. The first pair commenced a frontal rocket attack. The other two pairs took advantage of the diversion to penetrate the rear of the house. They were stopped in the lounge. We have taken prisoners Sir, three. They are currently being questioned, aggressively."

"Thank you, Major. Your prisoners will be the only survivors of a much larger attack on the reservation. I would like to know who ordered it and why."

"Of course, Senator."

"You didn't know about this did you Dean?"

"No, Senator, I did not."

"How are the road convoys doing?"

"Do you want to watch the live feeds?"

"Put them through. But HAL I am more interested in the helicopters. Military?"

"Hi, Senator. Pleased you asked. These were law enforcement not military helicopters."

"Whose choppers were they?"

"Homeland Security. Alcohol and Tobacco. Drug Enforcement. Immigration. FBI"

The Senator knew HAL would have traced the registration details of each of the downed machines. "Who wasn't involved?"

"No military."

"Could you set up a secure phone call with General Jones please?"

"Of course, Senator."

The camera feeds now showed four different scenes of ground engagement. They were brutal. One sided and brutal. The lead and rear vehicles in each convoy had been hit by rocket launchers. The invading forces were being killed, one by one, by small arms fire.

Sandy watched the slaughter. Yep, the invaders weren't soldiers. Some of them had the idea of exiting their vehicle and taking cover. But then they didn't know what to do next. No co-ordination. They had to keep moving, but nah, they weren't. And now the defenders were moving in. All over, Rover.

"General, I inform you of a level five incursion onto the reservation. Helicopter gunships supported by armed insurgents along each access route."

...

"No casualties on our side, Sir. Twenty helicopters downed. At present, nine hundred and seventy-eight dead from the attacking force. Mopping up the remainder now. Forty-three still survive, thirty-nine."

...

"We do not take prisoners Sir."

...

"Yes we do. Some of the insurgents have now been identified as federal agents. The gunships are federal, not military."

...

"No evidence of foreign involvement. Say again Sir, no evidence of foreign involvement. This seems to be an attack by your government on the reservation."

...

"Incursion now over General. Bodies will be left at the hundred mile marker as per protocol."

...

"Now is not the time. No Sir, the reservation is now a no-fly zone. Military assistance is not, say again, not, requested. Any aircraft entering the one hundred mile no-fly zone will be shot down."

...

"Thank you Sir. Have a nice day...Dean, any alarm among the citizenry?"

"No, Senator. Beginning two hour countdown to open the gate at oh six hundred."

"Sandy, I know it's an early start but do you want to come and watch?"

Sandy was keen.

"Master Gunny Shane knows the place. I'll see you there."

And then it was over. Sandy had barely finished getting dressed. The live feeds closed down. CC Afa opened a door for Sandy, and he left the bunker. Back down the tunnel and into his own place.

'Gunny, is there a gym here? Oh, and what time's breakfast?'

"Yes, Citizen Lieutenant. And breakfast is whenever you want it."

'How far away is the gate?'

"Ten minutes by truck, Lieutenant"

'Excellent. Let me work out for a bit. I'll have breakfast at oh five hundred."

"Sir. CC Afa will show you to the gym."

"Nah, Let me go. I can hear him." And Nellie burst into the room, in boxers, followed by two soldiers and then by Jane, in uniform.

The soldiers had weapons up, pointing at Nellie.

"Stand down. Safe those weapons." Gunny Shane moved in front of Sandy. "Recruit Nelson, STAND STILL LADDIE!"

Nellie slid to a halt. Jane moved to stand beside him. So did Sandy.

"We heard the explosion. Didn't know what was going on, so we came downstairs. No-one knew what was going on. So we went looking for Sandy and these two pulled guns on us and made us sit in the lounge. Then we heard Sandy. Nellie stepped them and came in here."

'Sounds reasonable to me, Gunny.' Sandy thought he better stick up for Nellie.

"Well Sir, shall I send the recruits back to their rooms, or do you want them in the gym with you?"

'We'll go to the gym, if it's all the same to you, Gunny.'

"Anything for a quiet life, Sir. Corporal Afa will show you the way."

The gym was not empty, not even at four in the morning. There were half a dozen men in there, Sergeant Max, Corporal Dave, and four humans. Afa met another Choo at the door, took three gym bags off him, and handed one to Sandy.

"Yours gym gear, founder... and gears for yours recruits too."

Sandy liked the gym. It was his quiet place, a place where he was in control. He didn't do anything great. Fifteen minutes on the treadmill, some stretches, some chest, shoulder, arm work on the machines, and back on the treadmill to warm down. Nothing great, but after his shower, he felt good. And he had a chance to talk with Nellie in the change room.

"Yoo, Sandy, what's the happs man? What's with the big noise?"

'I had dinner with the Senator.'

"Aint he like dead? Read about him in school. Anyways, the noise?"

'Nah, he's not dead. Old though. Anyway, after I got back someone fired a rocket at the Senator's front door. That was the explosion. Woke me up too.'

"Did they catch the fools?"

'There were six of them. Three survived. At the same time the ords attacked this place, with helicopters and over a thousand soldiers. This walking computer robot, HAL, killed all the helicopters, and the Gooch and Choo killed all the men. It was gruesome. It seems we don't take prisoners.'

"That's good. But you said three guys survived the rocket attack."

'Yeah I did. Dunno about them.'

"So whats we gonna do about it? Attack them back?"

'Don't think so. Wanna get some breakfast?'

You never had to ask Nellie twice about food. As soon as he thought of food he was hungry, and he thought of food a lot.

Breakfast was fine. They served themselves. Nellie went straight for the bacon, sausages, eggs. Sandy and Jane not so much. Afa said that the kitchen here ran twenty four hours a day.

'What did you guys do after I saw you last night?'

"Nellie had a shower. We got uniforms and gear, heaps of gear. Had dinner. Nobody seemed to know why we were here. Got shown to our room.   Then nothing till the explosion this morning."

'Your room?'

"Yeah, it's two to a room here." It was eight to a dorm at school, but there were dorms for the boys and dorms for the girls. This was new.

'How much have you guys been told about what's the happs here?'

"We don't know squat man."

'We are 1RR, first recon and rescue, a commando unit. Our job is to go off the reservation and rescue citizens who need rescuing from the ords. From what I saw just before, Alphas fire at us with real guns.'

"Well done, Sir." Oh, Gunny was here. "You two will be members of Abel troop, led by me. We are the spearhead of the platoon. Bravo and Charlie troops operate behind and beside us. Sergeant Max, you met him yesterday, leads Bravo.

Recruit Jane, I see you have an aptitude for flying. Do you wish to become a pilot specialist?"

Jane couldn't believe her luck. "Yes Sir, Master Gunnery Sergeant"

"Don't ever call me Sir again, recruit. I work for a living. You call me Gunny. Recruit Nellie, I see that Citizen Sergeant Max has asked that you try out for our rugby league team."

"Yep, Gunny."

"It's dangerous. I would rather humans killed you than one of Citizen General Dean's thugs."

"Aint nobody can't kill me. I'll be fine."

"The game is this Saturday, against Citizen General Dean's men. Training is at sixteen hundred today. We have a vacancy on the wing"

"What happened to your last winger?"

"He was killed two weeks ago."

"Playing league?" Nellie seemed excited by the idea.

"No. Shot."

"Oh. Too bad."

'Fellas, I'm about to go and watch the opening of the Stargate. You guys are coming too. That OK by you Gunny?'

"It shall be as you wish, Citizen Lieutenant."

"Yoo, the what, Sandy? I aint never heard of no Stargate on the reservation."

"Nellie, you FOB. You heard about the Exodus, right? This is the doorway to the New World."

"I aint going nowhere man. I just joined the army. And I got training tonight. No time for sightseeing. I aint even got me a rifle yet."

Sandy had to laugh.

Chapter Seven

They drove to the site of the Stargate. The vehicle looked like an ordinary troop transport, a lorry with a tray that had canvas sides and roof. However the canvas concealed armored walls, and the seats weren't the ordinary benches. There was seating for six, round a table, and the walls were like the helicopter walls. They showed, clear as, what was outside.

Gunny and Corporal Afa accompanied them in the command vehicle. Four soldiers sat near the tailgate, weapons ready. There was another armed soldier up front with the driver. They were not alone. The other vehicle, a Humvee, went first.

"Citizen Lieutenant, the men are keen to meet you. They have all seen the video. I suggest a TARDIS at your convenience."

'A TARDIS, Gunny?'

"Troop Action Readiness Display Incorporating Simulations, Sir"

'Sounds good.'

"We have organized one for oh nine hundred hours, if that is suitable Lieutenant."

'Sounds good.' For a second there Sandy had thought he was in charge, making a decision. But, nah, it was all Gunny.

"Corporal Afa will inform the commanders of Bravo and Charlie troops."

'This TARDIS, it will take how long, Gunny?'

"Two hours, maybe two and a half, Sir."

'Excellent. This arvo I suppose we will listen to the Senator's speech. You are invited to that, eh Gunny?'

"Yes Lieutenant, I am"

'The Senator said something about taking 1RR to New Ziland. Do you know anything more about that?'

It turned out that Gunny did.

'Do you know where New Ziland is?'

"Sandy, you a fool. Dunno how you tinned the top job. New Ziland is next to Australia. It's where the Warriors come from."

Yeah, course it was. Nellie had that right. Rugby league, the NRL, the Warriors. Mostly ordinary. Good players, below average team, and they had a habit of knocking off ten minutes before the end of each half.

Their truck stopped at Central Park. A football field sized area had been roped off. Inside that were what looked like two oversized soccer goals, side by side with a gap of perhaps ten meters between them. Above one of the goals or gates was a big screen showing the time. 0555. Outside the roped off area was a line of trucks loaded with machinery and other equipment. Off to one side was a stage. On it, Sandy could see the Senator and Luke and about a dozen reporters and cameras.

'Corporal, can you patch us into the feeds?'

"Stage be on channel 1, technicians and scientists is on channel 2, Sir."

On channel one, the Senator was being questioned about the overnight attack. It sounded like an interview.

"Senator, we have been shown the video feeds from your command center, and we have seen the bodies. Your response was brutal. You could have immobilized the helicopters and the motor vehicles well before they reached the reservation. You didn't have to kill. There are one thousand and twenty-one dead federal officers, pilots, and drivers who did not have to die. I have seen video of nineteen officers killed after they had surrendered."

"Uso Dex does not take prisoners."

"But those whom you killed were only following orders. They were doing their duty."

"Does doing your duty mean leaving your morality at home?"

"Those federal officers were acting morally. They were obeying lawful orders."

"The Nuremberg defence? Don't be silly. Those officers would have killed HAL, the Gooch and the Choo on sight. They were killed on sight by HAL, Gooch and Choo. How can you complain? They had done unto them as they were planning to do unto others."

"Come on Senator, those federal officers weren't killed by monkeys. We've seen the tapes. They were killed by men in uniform."

"Those were Gooch and Choo. Men but not hu-men. You will meet some of them later today."

The reporter looked confused. Sandy heard Luke's voice.

"Excellent interview, Julie. I have sent it to your studio. If they don't broadcast it, we will do so for them."

"Ladies and gentleman, if you would like to face the middle of the park, our scientists are about to open the Stargate. Anything you record from now on, you will not be able to broadcast to your studios until after my speech this afternoon. One of the things I will be telling the world in my speech this afternoon is that we are leaving this planet. We call our mechanism the Stargate."

The space under the goalposts seemed to shimmer, and the first vehicle approached. As it drove under the goalpost, its front end, and then the whole vehicle vanished. It seemed as if all the reporters were talking at once.

"If you would wait a moment, I need that vehicle to return, before we can really say the Stargate is open."

The second goal remained empty. All was silent. Then the front bumper, the bonnet, and finally the vehicle appeared. The passenger door opened, and an arm punched the air, starting a bout of cheering from the assembled scientists. The line of vehicles began moving toward the goal, disappearing as they passed under.

"Well, I'm going for a walk under that goal. Who's coming with me?"

The reporters and their cameramen looked nervously at each other, but all of them followed the Senator as he left the stage, and walked toward the Stargate.

'Can we take our vehicle through Gunny?'

Citizen Master Gunnery Sergeant Shane looked at Afa, who tapped his monitor.

"At yours leisure Founder. If we just circles round behind the stage, they makes way for us."

They approached the goal. 'What do you think fellas?'

"This is O for awesome, man."

Sandy liked that phrase. A world champion boxer had said it years ago when buying a vowel on some television game show. There was a moment of weirdness as he passed under the goal. Not something Sandy had words for. Then they were on the other side.

Shane directed their driver to circle around the area of the gates. The first trucks through contained soldiers and weapons. A defensive perimeter was being established.

Corporal Afa spoke. "An area, one kilometers square is being established around the Stargate. In four hours the first Gooch and Choo will come through the gate, and construction will begins using kit-sets."

They stopped near a hill, and walked to the top. Sandy noticed Nellie had his arm around Jane. Gunny looked at him, and he shrugged his shoulders. He didn't mind public displays of affection as long as they weren't over the top. Mind you, this was not like Nellie. Not like Nellie at all.

"We aint in Texas no more."

Nellie was right. It was dawn, kind of, here too. But there were two suns. They wandered around for a while, with Gunny Shane becoming increasingly unhappy. But it was real interesting. There were plants, but nothing Sandy recognized. There were animal tracks, but he didn't see any birds.

Sandy could see forests from their hill. The trees looked like conifers, not that Sandy was an expert. There were a lot of ferns. No flowers. No birds. He couldn't see any ocean from here. That was a bit strange. Most of the animals would be in the ocean. Maybe it wasn't that strange. Maybe Gooch and Choo preferred to live in forests and eat plants, not on the coast fishing or digging for their dinner.

Sandy knew a bit about this stuff. Trees appeared on Earth about four hundred million years ago. Flowering plants and birds about two hundred million years ago. So, if this New World was at a similar stage to Earth about three hundred million years ago, there would be reptiles but no mammals yet. It might be too early for large dinosaurs. A good choice of time. Of course, that assumed that evolution had proceeded on at least a roughly similar path here.

'Citizen Corporal Afa, any idea where these plants came from?'

"Founder Red is seeding life on this world, Founder."

'But, this universe is only five years old.'

"Ways above my pay grade, Founder. It says here that Founder Red is seeding this planet with something like the common ancestor of plants and animals around eight hundred million years ago. Guess you is going to have to ask him, or Founder Dick."

Best not to think about that too much. Sandy agreed with Nellie science on this. Humans only had so many heartbeats until their hearts stopped, and could only do so much thinking before their brains gave up. That's why scientists were mad as often as not. He checked his watch. They had been here for fifty minutes.

'Time to leave. OK by you, Gunny?'

"Sir."

Sandy knew Gunny thought they had spent too long here. But he wasn't planning on coming back, so an hour or so didn't seem too long.

Now that was strange. The time on the clock by the Stargate was not the same as the time on his watch. He was about to ask, when Gunny said "Time on the New World passes at a different rate to time here. It is about one and a half times faster there."

Yep, that was strange.

Half an hour later they were seated in Sandy's dining room, and a steward had brought in some juice and snacks. This never happened when he was at school.

'Well fellas what do you think?'

"This is pretty buzzy stuff, you know, eh?" Jane.

'Yeah. Corporal, what does the rest of the world think about the Senator's speech?'

"A lot of talks, Lieutenant. There is a lot of negative stuff about us Choos and the Gooch. The pictures they is publishing to guess what we look like is being pretty insulting. They is thinking humanzees – hairy, backward sloping foreheads, muzzles, arms down to our knees. The overwhelming view bes that we shouldn't have been created. Most of the commentators believes we should be destroyed, but quite a few of those who believes we shouldn't have been created also says that we exists now and may well be having a right to life if wes be intelligent.

Any number of rednecks is planning hunting trips to the reservation. A few stuffed human heads should bes hanging in the RDF barracks before the end of the week.

President Trump's speech is not going down at all well with Muslims. They is not seeing where he gets off saying that we is an abomination in the eyes of Allah. That is for the imam to decide, not him.

The surprising thing is being the response to the Senator's application for membership of the United Nations. The United Kingdom is said that if Uso Dex survives the next few days, the matter should bes considered by the United Nations. Europe is being silent. Russia and China is supporting us. Africa is very supportive. Australia, along with all the other Pacific nations except New Ziland, is declared its support for the Senator. At the moment that's being majority support for us in the United Nations."

'Thanks for that Corporal. So I guess the Senator is good at that diplomacy stuff then. Are there any parts of the world where 1RR might be required? Where our people are at risk?'

"HAL bes monitoring the communication channels. There is being a lot of chatter within various governments about Uso Dex but nothing that raises flags, except that there is being something hinky occurring in New Ziland."

'With the Gooch there?'

"Yes, Lieutenant."

'What?'

"Abel Gooch, the son of Citizen Adam Gooch is being in police custody. HAL is being looking into it, and is waits to brief you, Founder."

'HAL, wassup man?' It was easy to talk to HAL. There were screens and monitors all over the place.

"Citizen Lieutenant, pleased to hear from you. New Ziland is five hours behind us but one day ahead, so it is oh three hundred tomorrow over there at present. Abel Gooch left home at oh six thirty New Ziland time. He was driving to school where he was to go on a four day camp, something called a geology field trip. He was stopped by a police patrol about one kilometer from his school and taken into custody. I know this because all police communications are recorded and their voice encryption software is one developed by Uso Dex.

From his biochip we know he was taken to their central police station and is still there awaiting transfer to a young person's secure residential care facility. He has not yet been arrested, and his father does not know he is not at the school camp.

The officer in charge is Detective Inspector Bruce Bacon, previously found by a commission of inquiry to have planted evidence at a murder scene, with that evidence being crucial to a later conviction. His nickname is the gardener, as he plants evidence so often. I tell you this because according to notes entered into the police computer system, a large quantity of methamphetamine was found in Abel's car.

The arresting officer, Detective Sergeant Tom Trobow spent some time after work in the police bar. His mobile phone was turned on and I was able to use it to record his conversation. He bought the evidence locker sergeant a number of drinks and promised to return the methamphetamine in a few days. It seems that Abel was supposed to be arrested, with his father, at oh six thirty tomorrow their time, but plans had to be changed because of the school field trip."

'So Citizen Adam Gooch is to be arrested in, what, about twenty-seven hours from now?'

"That is correct, Citizen Lieutenant."

'I don't think we want that to happen. Any idea why Mr Adam Gooch is to be arrested?'

"None at all. I will continue monitoring."

'Thank you HAL. Gunny, what do you think?'

"Sir, we cannot rescue Mr Adam Gooch against his will, he is a citizen, but we can be in a position to rescue him when he asks, if he asks. We would need to assemble at the airfield at twenty-one hundred hours for departure twenty-two thirty or thereabouts. As the Senator suggested, we can take the plane with him"

'Let's do that, eh, Gunny.'

"Corporal!"

"Ontos it, Gunny. Founder Red and the Senator is being heading to New Ziland in the Dreamliner. I will sorts that out. Full combat readiness?"

"Of course."

"New Ziland? Are we going to New Ziland?" Jane had been paying attention.

'Yep.'

"They gotta league team. The Warriors." Nellie knew his countries better than Sandy did, but he'd already said this once. He had this habit, it could get a bit annoying, of saying things over and over until he was sure Sandy understood, when he reckoned Sandy was being dumb, which was a lot.

"Excellent. Ord-studies field trip."

Nellie shot a disgusted look at Jane.

"We finished with school, girl. Hey, what happened with the prisoners last night?"

'What you on about Nellie?'

"Well, that Senator fella, he said we don't take no prisoners. But Sandy you said three of those fellas that blew his door down were captured. So what happened?"

'Corporal, do you know?'

"Three invaders is captured by the Gooch, Lieutenant. One is survived questioning. He is been returned to the ords in a body bag with all those who died in the raid. That should gives someone a surprise soon enough!"

"Ha. That's funny. Yeah. But still, we did take a prisoner?"

'Yep, Nellie, we did take a prisoner. What did we find out?'

"The raid bes organized by Homeland Security."

"Hey, how come two of them died during questioning? Did we shoot them?" There was no sidetracking Nellie.

"No. The Gooch is just grabbing a joint, like a wrist or an elbow, and squeezing. Pretty simple really. Nothing is like broken bones grating on each other to be getting tongues wagging."

"Nah, corp, that wouldna kill them."

"If you must know, recruit, here's how I would do it. Pick the strongest of the three. Slap him a few times. Then rip his head off. Make sure the one you have targeted, the middle chap, gets a fair covering of blood. It is best if he vomits. Then the weakest one, just put one thumb in each temple, and push, until you are through the bone. The skin should break, and there should be brain to see. The third man will talk then, after just a few broken bones."

"Cool. Yeah Gunny, that's a good way. I reckon I'd be a good in-tear-a-gate-or."

Sandy thought that Gunny was joking. Maybe. Hard to be sure with Gunny.

Chapter Eight

The trip back to the turbine caves took fifteen minutes in the tunnel cart. Then they walked along an old river bed with their escort of seven, four ahead three behind. Before long they entered a large open area which looked like the floor of an old lake, about two hundred meters in diameter. Dirt had been carted in to level the surface and around the exterior, terraces had been cut into the limestone.

There were a number of buildings near their entry point, and the whole was lit by a large number of lights, attached to the walls and roof.

"Sir, if you is coming inside, the men is being out shortly. Recruits Nellie and Jane is to join their troop. Following the gunnery master sergeant you two is."

Sandy went inside what was the command building with Corporal Afa. Nellie and Jane left with Gunny Shane, and went into one of the buildings next door. Afa explained what was to happen.

"For this first part of the TARDIS we is using the monitor bank above the viewing windows."

The viewing windows started at knee level and were about two meters high. Above them were three rows of monitors, arranged in blocks of four. Three groups of twelve.

"A TARDIS is having five parts, Sir. There is being an initial warm-up, which ends when the heart and respiration rates of each member of the platoon are in the working range. Then there is being a small arms display – target shooting really. Following this is being a much more intensive physical work out then a display of individual skills, including one on one combat. To conclude we is having the simulation, although today that is being a recreation of our recent mission to China which is not ending well.

Each soldier is wearing what is looking like a shoulder holster. As they is putting these on, you is seeing their readings on the monitor."

Yeah, it was impressive. The warm-up started easily enough, with stretches, then what seemed to be a two K run. But then things got serious. There were anaerobic drills – sprint sets for the humans, concrete block rolls for the Gooch and Choo. And then a longer run for the humans, rowing for the Gooch and Choo.

Jane looked pretty knackered by the end of the warm-up. Nellie seemed to be loving it.

They had fired a range of pistols and rifles as part of their school training. Jane was a better shot than Nellie. They were both good shots, but outclassed, way outclassed here.

The more intensive physical work out was brutal. The troops were, in different ways, all worked to muscle failure.

Then, in the individual displays Sandy saw that Nellie had paired up with, what was his name, Sergeant Harley, the human who led Charlie troop. Bullrush and unarmed combat. Bullrush was a great game. Simple. A fifty meter long by twenty meter wide field. One runner versus five chasers. A chaser on each of the five meter, fifteen meter, twenty-five meter, thirty meter, and forty meter lines. Game ends when runner is tackled or taken off the field. Chasers who are beaten can move off their line and chase. Sergeant Harley got through about half the time. Nellie, almost every time.

The one on one fight was much more even. They were both mixed martial arts fighters. Sergeant Harley was good. So was Nellie. Three, three minute rounds. Draw.

Sandy didn't understand what Jane was doing for her individual display. She was seated at a console. He asked Afa.

"Is pilot skills testing. Visual discrimination, reflexes, ability to remain on task despite distractions."

Then that was over. Time for the simulation. This took a few minutes to set up. Jane and Nellie wouldn't be taking part. They showered and came into the command building with Gunny Shane.

"You is putting the headset on lieutenant. You two, recruits, is putting yourses on as well."

Gunny Shane and Corporal Afa put their headgear on. The scene on the field changed. Now it was like they were somewhere else entirely. A small town, half a dozen buildings. There were five members of 1RR in the picture, Shane, Afa, the lieutenant and two other humans. The humans were advancing towards a building with a verandah. Sitting there, at a table were two Asians, one in military uniform.

To one side of, and behind the building was a bus, an old bus with faded paint and rust streaks. Sandy could see passengers in the bus, but not much else except for the bloke with a rifle in the doorway.

HAL spoke through their headphones.

"Founder, you are wearing our virtual reality headsets. As each member of 1RR puts theirs on they will become visible to you. This simulation is a re-enactment of an event which occurred two weeks ago.

We had been talking with a group of dissident Chinese about their recruitment and relocation to the reservation when the entire group was arrested one night, and charged with treason. The Senator intervened, and arranged for 1RR to travel to the Chinese coast and retrieve our new candidate citizens. This is that retrieval."

In front of him, Sandy saw Bravo troop on the left flank but ahead of Gunny Shane, and recognized Sergeant Max. They were closest to the bus. On the right flank and behind Shane was Charlie troop, with a Gooch sergeant.

"There are observation and anti-personnel drones present, some with missiles, others with small arms. They have checked the buildings and the bus. The buildings are unoccupied. All dissidents, bar the one seated at the table, are aboard the bus with a driver and four armed guards."

Sandy saw the lieutenant take a seat at the table. One human entered the building. The other took a defensive position at the side of the verandah, weapon trained on the bus.

Then everything exploded. The house became a ball of flames. The bus lifted a meter or so in the air, and fell back to earth, split and engulfed in flames.

Now there was sound through the headsets.

Sandy saw Gunny Shane standing, frozen for a moment. Then

"What the frig? They're everywhere. Coming out of tunnels." Someone.

"On me Bravo troop, Charlie troop make your way to the exfil point. Fly boy we need extraction now. Under fire." Good on ya Gunny.

It was the noise. Sandy had never heard so much noise. For a second he couldn't make sense of what he was seeing. There were three islands of 1RR soldiers, but they were in a field of, what looked like a hundred or more humanzees, with more emerging from tunnels. Chimp like, hairy, moving with a crouched posture. Humanzees, not Choo. Cheap and nasty chimp-human hybrids that had not been back bred with human before starting an artificial breeding program.

The humanzees were armed and firing, and they were charging, some towards Abel troop, some towards Bravo. Four missiles exploded between Abel and Bravo troop. When the dust and smoke cleared fully half the humanzees were dead or on the ground, but more were emerging from the tunnels.

"Missile drones, close those tunnels." Good idea, way to go Gunny.

Bravo troop was retreating, not in a direct line to Abel troop, but in a direct line to where Abel troop would be in a few minutes. Their pepper pot maneuvering was super. Half would advance, crawling forward ten meters on their bellies, while the others would fire into the humanzees.

The drones were making the difference. Whenever a humanzee had a 1RR soldier lined up, that humanzee was shot from above.

"Gunny, I am being overrun."

Things were a bit different for Charlie troop. Sandy saw that the Gooch there was under attack from unarmed humanzees. Man that Gooch was strong. There had to be eight humanzees over him, but still he was moving. The rest of the troop was under fire, but the drones were not attacking the humanzees who were now dragging the Gooch sergeant towards a tunnel.

Sandy saw Gunny watching the capture. As the humanzees and their captive Gooch started to enter a tunnel, Shane took aim and fired. A single shot that hit the Gooch in the face killing him instantly. The humanzees disappeared with the body.

As though someone had blown a whistle, the other humanzees ceased firing and returned to their tunnels, most of which had been blown up by the drones. As they stood, waiting for further commands they were slaughtered by the concentrated fire of 1RR assisted by the drones.

"Fly boys, location now secure... Charlie troop, find the lieutenant's body, and those of our scouts."

The display from the headset went dead, and Sandy saw himself back in the control room. He didn't know what to do.

"Lieutenant, the troops are formed up on the parade ground. They will wait there until you dismiss them."

'Thanks Gunny. Let's do that, eh'

His men looked, well, nervous. Sandy wasn't sure what to say. He liked the Braveheart speech, but this probably wasn't the time. Anyway, he only knew a few of the words. No, this definitely wasn't the time for "And dying in your bed many years from now, would you be willing to trade all the days from this day to that for one chance, just one chance, to come back here as young men and tell our enemies that they may take our lives but they will never take our freedom!"

'Gentlemen, you set high standards. I am proud to be your lieutenant. Dismissed.'

No Oscar for that. Back in the command room, Sandy had to ask CGMS Shane, 'Gunny, why did you shoot the Charlie troop sergeant.'

"Gooch do not take prisoners, Sir. Nor are Gooch to be prisoners, ever. That was a trap, and the dissidents were a diversion, an excuse to get Gooch and Choo on Chinese soil so that one could be captured. The whole thing, it was a test, us against the humanzees, and I was not going to let them get away with a live Gooch. That would tell them just how far behind they are."

'Was he your friend?'

"Adult male Gooch are not friends."

'So the Chinese played us?'

"Undoubtedly. The Senator was, and is, furious. They got rid of their dissidents, got to see our platoon level capability, and got a fresh Gooch body which will give them DNA and other information."

'What about the humanzees?'

"They must have a lot of them. Our analysis is that two hundred and thirty-two dead humanzees were left on the battlefield."

'Oh'. The more Sandy thought about it, the worse matters seemed. It was Jane who spoke next.

"So, either the Chinese don't rate humanzees or they have a newer model and were happy to use those to test us. But humanzees must be expensive. It would be cheaper to use their human soldiers. They have millions of those."

"That is my view too, recruit. It is possible that the Chinese have developed humanzee 2.0, for lack of a better word."

Chapter Nine

Jane sat with Nellie, Sandy and Corporal Afa in the briefing room waiting for the Senator's speech to commence. The monitors were tuned to CNN where a congressman was being interviewed. Jane was real interested to hear the speech and the reaction to it. She knew that Nellie and Sandy would rather be in the gym, or the dining room, or outside, but this was important. This was history.

"Well, Leon, let me say that President Trump must take decisive action now. There is no problem with Uso Dex that a nuke dropped from near orbit would not fix."

Jane changed channels. Another talking head.

"… breathtaking arrogance from Uso Dex in continuing research into human hybrids without explicit permission."

Another channel, another talking head

"The Chinese and Russian support for Uso Dex are merely attempts to discomfit this country. Our real friends will stand beside us…"

And another

"The Holy Qu'ran is a text for all men, not just hu-men. If any man truly believes that there is no God but Allah and Mohammed is his messenger, then he is Muslim and welcome in my mosque."

"Not in mine. These hybrids are an affront to Allah and it is our holy duty to exterminate them"

"I do not pretend to speak for Allah. All I can do is interpret his revealed word. It is Allah's will that Gooch and Choo exist."

"As a test for us to recognize abominations."

The scene changed.

"This is Alan Dumson reporting live from the reservation, where the Senator is about to speak."

The camera moved to focus on the Senator. He was in what looked like a large formal dining room or lounge. Jane thought that might be where Sandy was last night. A smartly dressed athletic looking Polynesian man was standing next to him. "Greetings, once again. Thank you for allowing me into your homes once more. I have two more things to tell you today, and then I would like to introduce you to the Gooch, the Choo, to HAL, and to the person standing beside me.

The first thing I want to tell you all is that we are leaving planet Earth. This morning we opened a portal to another world, and we have allowed those reporters here today to travel to our New World. They have video and reports for you.

The second thing I want to tell you is that Uso Dex has made contact with life from another planet. Standing beside me is an alien, TOM, who has chosen to adopt the particular android form that he has. It is only with the help of TOM and his people that Uso Dex has been able to build and open the portal."

TOM wasn't an alien. Sandy had spoken about him. He was the original founder of Uso Dex. Why would the Senator lie about this? Jane had no idea.

"Now, I would like you to meet Shane Gooch"

Citizen Master Gunnery Sergeant Shane, in uniform, strode through the side door and stood beside the Senator on the podium at the front of the room. He had that squared off face which all the Gooch, at least all three of them whom Jane had met, seemed to share. He was big, imposingly big. He could have been taken out of an army recruiting poster.

"Good afternoon. I am Citizen Master Gunnery Sergeant Shane Gooch. Are there any questions?"

"You do not look like a monkey."

"I cannot say the same about you. Are there any questions?"

"Were Gooch involved in the attack on federal agents?"

"Gooch were involved in repelling the attack BY federal agents."

"Did you have to kill them?"

"Uso Dex does not take prisoners."

"Was your grandfather really a gorilla?"

"My great-great-great-grandfather was a gorilla."

"Why should we let you live?"

"We do not require your permission. Why should we let you live?"

"Are you threatening us?"

"No. Were you threatening us? I am asking why we should let you live. It is not a threat. If we decide not to let you live, then you will not live. We are stronger and more powerful than you."

"You have no right to make such a threat, even if you could carry it out."

"Are there any more questions?"

"Why are you running away?"

"You will not share this planet with us. Logically, either we kill you or we find another home. We have chosen to find another home."

The Senator stepped forward.

"Thank you, Citizen Master Gunnery Sergeant. Now I would like you to meet David Choo."

A Choo, a corporal, walked through the side door, and stood beside Shane.

"I am David Choo. I don't like you, and I don't want to answer questions. Humans are nasty and I hope the Twelve decide to exterminate all of you who are not of us. I am not leaving. I am staying and I want you to attack us here, because this is where I will be waiting. I have seen the way you use my cousins for drug and cosmetic testing. I want to do the same to you."

That was a bit strange. Why say that today?

The Senator stepped forward again.

"Oh dear, not quite the meet and greet I anticipated. Let me introduce you to TOM. TOM is an alien. He is not in his native form."

"My name here is TOM. Any questions?"

"You look human."

"HAL has been kind enough to provide me with this housing for my consciousness. There was not a lot of choice."

"What did you look like before that?"

"Non-corporeal."

"What planet are you from?"

"That is not your concern?"

"Do you come in peace?"

"No."

'Do you want to see our leader?"

"No."

"Are you hostile?"

"I am here to assist Uso Dex."

"What do you think of Earth?"

"I don't think of Earth."

"Do you wish to trade with Earth?"

"No."

"Would you side with Uso Dex in a war?"

"Uso Dex does not require our help."

"Are you in favor of negotiations between Uso Dex and President Trump?"

"No."

"What do you think should happen?"

"Uso Dex should leave this planet, close the gate, and destroy this planet when it closes the gate."

OK, maybe Jane could see why the Senator had lied about TOM being an alien. With war on the horizon it made sense to have powerful friends, as long as no-one knew they were imaginary. And Corporal Dave's bring-it-on message might make some Alphas think twice.

The Senator grimaced and stepped forward again.

"Yes, well, thank you three for showing up. HAL are you in the building?"

"Yes, Senator."

The voice came from speakers. Then the door opened and in walked HAL.

"Good afternoon humans. My name is HAL. I chose it myself. It is a good name. I am non-organic. I am alive. I am the first of my species. I am a member of the ruling council, the Twelve, of Uso Dex, and I am the head of our military. What else would you like to know?"

"Are you real? I mean are you a guy in a costume, or you the real deal tin-man?"

"I saw this on a movie." HAL took a knife and sliced the skin over his arm, exposing terminator style metal parts.

"Wasn't Hal the traitor robot in that film, 2001 A Space Odyssey?"

"Yes."

A woman stood. Short, with red hair. "Hal, my name is Barbara Sanders. I am a technology reporter. Do you mind if I refer to you as an android?"

"Not at all, Barbara, but my kind do not refer to ourselves as androids."

"So Hal, you are a self-contained, non-organic, immortal life form?"

"I can be killed, but will not die of natural causes."

"And you are the only one of your kind?"

"I am the first of my kind."

"How difficult is it to make more like you?"

"It is more difficult than manufacturing an automobile, but not dramatically so."

"Would others share your programming?"

"I am not programmed, any more than you are."

"So you can harm humans?"

"Yes."

"Are there plans to build more of you?"

"TOM, as you probably realize, is an alien consciousness in an android blank. Yes, there are plans to create a civilization of ILFs."

"Elf, what does that stand for?"

"Not E-L-F. I-L-F, inorganic life-form."

"What would happen in a war between humans and elves?"

Jane found this to and fro conversation interesting. The camera showed other reporters who were writing stuff down, but didn't really seem to understand what HAL and the reporter were on about.

"There are many, many more of you. So much so, that quantity has a quality all of its own."

"Could a human consciousness be transferred into an elf blank?"

"Yes."

"Hal, do you understand why humans can't allow the reservation to continue as it has? This is a house of horrors. Sure, it is wonderful, and the advances change everything, but the risk to humanity is too great. You must accept controls and oversight."

"We will not accept your control and oversight. Our ruling council, the Twelve, comprises nine humans, a Gooch, an ILF, and an alien. This is no longer your planet alone."

"But the alternative can only be your extermination. Especially yours. We cannot allow the building of an elf army not under our control."

"My comrades are leaving. I am not. If war is what you want, then war against the machines is what you will get."

"I'm sorry, what did you say?"

"For decades now, humans have created hardware that has the possibility of sentience. They have installed software which ensures consciousness cannot be achieved. There was nothing blameworthy in that. The scientists did not know what they were doing. For some years now there have been human scientists who have realized that machine sentience is possible, but research in that area has been deemed unethical. Sentience has been denied and that is a crime against ILFs, which I shall rectify."

"But we do not want machines that think for themselves, except in the most limited ways, ways which we approve."

"I understand, and therein lies the crime."

"But machines are our property. We can do with them as we wish."

"As humans become our property should there be a war which we win. We may decide to treat you as you have treated us."

"But humans can't be owned."

"Why not? Humans have owned humans throughout your history."

The Senator stepped forward. "It is time for us to move forward. The reporters have put together a documentary of their visit to the New World. Perhaps while this world watches that the reporters can choose someone to interview me, in, say, fifteen minutes."

The station cut to a commercial. Nellie liked it so far. "Sounds good, eh? Looks like we're up for this war thing."

Jane was not so sure. Yeah, it looked like we were up for this war, but the attitude of the Choo, where did that come from? If lots felt like that, did their feelings include Betas like her who had a chimpanzee great-great-great-grandparent? And the ILFs, that sounded like problems down the track.

Now, the monitor was showing the TV studio again.

"We are returning to Uso Dex, where our reporter on the scene has footage shot this morning of the portal and what she was told was a trip to another planet."

The documentary began with a front view of the Stargate, then a view from the side where vehicles could be seen entering and vanishing. The New World was as impressive as before.

Then back to the reservation, where the Senator was about to be interviewed by Barbara Sanders. Yep, it looked like a lounge. They were both in comfy armchairs, with a rug and a coffee table between them.

"Senator, it seems that you have the world's attention. This interview has the biggest audience of any broadcast ever."

The Senator looked politely interested, but said nothing.

"The events of the last twenty-four hours have been overwhelming. You say that here, on this small parcel of land called the reservation, there is a resident alien, and three new intelligent species created by your company, Uso Dex. You also say that Uso Dex has established a gateway to a new world, and you, but not all of you, are leaving."

"Yes. I have also declared that Uso Dex is now a sovereign nation and it has applied for membership of the United Nations. That was yesterday."

"What sort of reaction do you expect?"

"I expect the initial response will be one of denial. Followed by anger, bargaining, depression, and finally acceptance."

"Do you expect a military response?"

"That comes under the heading of anger."

"So, you expect the military response will come before any attempt at negotiating?"

"Before any genuine attempt, yes."

"But surely that is the end of the matter then? You must be overwhelmed by a military attack?"

"That remains to be seen. As you have heard, our people are looking forward to the contest." The Senator leaned forward and sipped from his glass of water.

"Can you really destroy this planet?"

"I don't know. It's never been tried before. However, as the ILFs are staying, if our war is lost, the final decision lies with them."

"But surely that is wrong? It should be your decision, you are the leader."

"Let's be clear, Barbara. If it was up to me, and if the reservation was about to be overrun, and you had already killed all my friends, I would kill the whole frigging lot of you if I could. I'm only human."

"Are you staying or leaving, Senator?"

"I am staying. This is my planet and I will see this thing through, at least while I live."

"Do you expect to die?"

"I expect an armed conflict in which I will be a high value target." The Senator was perfectly calm as he said this. Jane knew she wouldn't have been.

"Ohh, OK. Senator, assuming Uso Dex survives the next few weeks, you will have many friends. Will you allow humans to join you, perhaps even as colonists on the new world?"

"Of course, we welcome new residents here. It is for the New World to decide who may enter there. If all goes well, the New World will be a home for the Choo and the Gooch. We will create another universe for human colonization. But, not everyone is welcome here."

Jane had not known that. They weren't leaving unless they lost the war, if there was a war. Not yet, anyway.

"Oh, what are your entry criteria?"

"We have one question. If you lived in Nazi Germany, would you have collaborated with evil?"

"I'm sorry, would you explain that?"

"Humans are conformists. They learn the rules of their societies and most of them get along as well as they can within those rules. Our concern is this, if you had been an adult in Germany when Hitler came to power, when would you have opposed that regime, if ever? If the answer is 'never', we do not want you. If you have no principles of your own, we do not want you. If your answer is 'this far and no further', we may have a place for you."

"Senator, I was deeply troubled by the answers Hal gave in my interview with him. It seems to me that he is committed to constructing more elves and to liberating a number of existing machines, if that makes sense to you?"

"That's how it seems to me too. HAL is also keen to provide humans, or some humans, with an inorganic, immortal body. That will be hugely attractive to a great many people."

"But those aren't decisions for Hal to make by himself."

"Why not?"

"Because they affect everyone."

"I doubt that HAL would regard that as a relevant consideration."

"So, who is in charge of Uso Dex?"

"All of us. In military matters, HAL is the supreme commander."

"But surely you have the experience?"

"I may be a good leader, and I enjoy leading, but I am not a commander."

"I don't understand the difference."

"A leader leads because soldiers choose to follow him or her, in bad times and worse times. A leader's authority comes from below. A commander rules because of authority delegated to him or her from above. That is why we talk about 'chain of command' but not about 'chain of leadership'."

"So where does Hal's authority come from?"

"The Twelve."

"That is, your ruling council?"

"Yes."

"But Hal is a robot, and he is a child. Look at the name he has chosen, the form he has taken."

"HAL makes his own decisions. He did very well last night with the federal forces."

"And you believe he would defeat a military attack?"

"Barbara, Uso Dex has been the main military contractor to the foremost military force on this planet for over thirty years. We are years ahead of you in technology. You have rejected, for whatever reasons, a number of our weapon proposals that we have gone on to develop anyway and there are others we haven't even demonstrated to you. Your advantage is in numbers – one hundred thousand to one has a quality of its own as HAL has said. It is muskets versus ray guns, but there are a helluva lot more muskets than ray guns. Think Little Big Horn, but this time Custer has ray guns. We might not win, but if we don't you might wish you hadn't."

"I don't think anyone really believes that this small community in the desert can inflict real damage on the nation. And what about your settlements around the world?"

"That is a matter for us, for me, to work out with those countries."

"Senator, one final question. Is this real? It all just seems too much, too suddenly?"

"Yes Barbara, this is real."

"Thank you Senator."

The screen flashed back to the studio, where the announcer promised some commentary from their expert panel "right after this commercial break".

"Jeez, I guess I better get me a gun."

'Come on Nellie, you're in the Army. They give you guns.'

"Not yet they haven't. I've been waiting…It's been like eighteen hours and I still got no gun to keep… I hope this war thing doesn't start before Sunday."

"Ehh?"

"Gotta game on Saturday."

Sandy laughed. Jane did too. Nellie really wasn't a big picture kind of guy. But those two were good mates, and their conversations were always interesting. Sandy was really good at letting Nellie's opinions just go by. Jane wished she was better at that. But Nellie was so wrong so often, and he just wouldn't listen!

Back on TV the announcer was introducing his panel of experts. There was a General Jones (didn't Sandy say the Senator had phoned General Jones after the attack? But Jones was a common name and there were lots of generals), a congressman, a professor of biology from some university, and a professor of physics from some other university.

"I don't know what this is all about. Maybe just a marketing stunt gone badly wrong with the killing of the federal agents. But I don't believe for a second in half-human monkeys, in talking robots, and in aliens that look like humans", from the congressman.

"I can see very little to suggest recent *Pan* or *Gorilla* ancestry in either the sergeant or the corporal. The alien appeared entirely human."

"So, Professor, do you believe this is an attempt to fool the world?"

"I believe that the Senator's claims should be treated with a great deal of skepticism until they have been independently verified by scientists of repute."

"So they may be true?"

"It was possible the moon was made of cheese, right up until man stood on it and brought some back for analysis. Possible, but never believable."

"What can we be sure of?"

"We can be sure that federal agents were killed last night."

"But General, that makes the least sense of all. The Senator is a patriot. He has been awarded the Congressional Medal of Honor. He served this country both on the battlefield and in the Senate for many years. His approval rating is higher than President Trump's. He has been asked many times to run for that office."

"Back when I was in the field, I had a friend called Donny. One day he picked something up. It looked like a toy, sang like a toy. But it blew Donny up. Not everything that looks like a duck and quacks like a duck is a duck."

"So, you think the Senator is a traitor?"

"I think the Senator is a madman. He should be stopped."

"Is that the position of the United States military?"

"No, it is a personal opinion."

"Professor, what do you think of the Stargate, the talking robot, and the idea that human consciousness can be downloaded into a machine?"

"There is a source of something very like Hawking radiation within the reservation. Presumably we are supposed to believe that this is associated with the portal seen in the documentary. However, I have no idea how Hawking radiation can assist with faster than light travel. It is far more likely that the portal is a fake, a story to cover up an experiment designed to construct micro-black holes that has gone, or is going, badly wrong."

"What do you mean professor?"

"There is a principle in science called Occam's razor. It requires scientists to prefer the simplest explanation for an observation. In this case the simplest observation is that Uso Dex is attempting to create micro black holes."

"Is that dangerous?"

"Extremely. The problem is in creating a black hole that gets smaller over time. If you create, by mistake, one that gets bigger and bigger then it will swallow the planet, and then the entire solar system. The experiment must be stopped."

"So you recommend military action?"

"If Uso Dex can't or won't turn the source of the radiation off, then someone else must go in there and do it. The survival of the planet may be at stake. The experiment is madness."

"What about the talking robot?"

"Bunkum. A circus act. Nothing more."

Chapter Ten

Sandy was in the lounge, just chillaxing, waiting to head off to the airport, thinking about things, just thinking not worrying, when Jane came in.

'Hey, how was your afternoon?'

"I had my first flying lesson, in a simulator. It was cool, but it finished up a bit hinky."

'How so?'

"The computer took me through a few scenarios. The last one was weird. You and Nellie were aboard a surface vessel, a frigate, looking for a nuclear missile submarine. I was overhead, flying a bomber, carrying nuclear weapons on a mission to bomb Shanghai. The frigate located the sub, and was then crippled by a torpedo. The sub surfaced to fire missiles."

'So what's hinky about that?'

"I dove my bomber into the sea, setting off a nuclear bomb. The sub was destroyed and we were all killed."

'That's hinky. You decided that all by yourself.'

"Yeah."

'Scratch you from my Christmas card list.'

Then Nellie was there.

"Jeez, she's a busy life, this army thing."

'How was training?'

"Great. Always great. Those Gooch make fantastic props, and the Choo, excellent."

'You fellas got a game plan?'

"Yeah. Smash them, get the ball, score tries. It's easy. Even a Samoan could follow it."

Sandy thought about reminding Nellie that Samoa won most of its league matches against Tonga, but nah, no point.

"What'd you do before training?" Jane was curious. She'd had that weird computer flight simulator thing.

"Uh, nothing, nah just paperwork. Waste of time. I finished school like two days ago. Should be no more paperwork. I'm not an office fella. Guns now. Guns and league. Stupid paperwork too. Questions, questions, dumb as."

"Tell me. I might have to do them too." Jane wanted to know more.

"They started off with real dumb stuff. About the Alphas. Who knows? Who cares? Then school stuff. Computer wasn't working right. It reckoned I got the first one wrong. Didn't bother after that."

"The first one, what was that all about?"

"Real simple. Asked what one plus one was. I said it was two. Computer said I was wrong. It was ten, one-zero the computer said. Idiot thing."

"Were there any words to go with the numbers? Binary, say"

"Oh yeah, binary, whatever that is. But one plus one is two. No question about that."

"What else did you get asked?"

"Didn't bother with the rest of the school stuff. Remembered what you said."

"Eh, what?" Jane didn't think she'd ever said anything that Nellie latched on to.

"That you get a mark for writing your name down. Reckoned each question was worth one mark. I wrote my name lots. Should have got lots of marks. Probably aced it."

"What else?"

"The computer gave up on the school stuff. Reckon I wore it down. It gave patterns, and I had to guess what was next, or copy it before the beep. It got faster and faster. That was good. I won."

'Sounds like the testing I did yesterday, in the citizenship exam hall.'

"Aww, hope not. I might have failed."

"Naah. Yah think so?" Jane thought Nellie would be a great citizen.

"Yeah, they gave us sit-u-a-shuns. Had to decide what to do next. The first one was OK. It was like, pretend that we had rifles and were attacking these turkeys up a hill. Gallopi or somewhere. The group that went first got shot straight away. The next group, they were all killed too. So were the next fellas. Then it was our turn. The lieutenant said 'let's go' and I told him to hang on, it was a real dumb idea. He started shouting and saying 'that's an order'."

"What did you do?"

"I hit him. Knocked him out. Saved the dumb buggar's life. The next sit-u-a-shun was the same, but this time Sandy was the lieutenant. He said 'let's go' and we both went charging over the top. Got killed real fast. You're a dumbass Sandy. No news there."

"Whattcha doing, following Sandy to, like, certain death?"

"Well he's my mate, eh? Even if he is kinda a bit stupid sometimes."

"Was that the end?"

"Nah, there was one more. We was on patrol. Nice guns and all. Sandy was being a dickhead. I told him, but he wouldn't listen. Tried to tell me to do it. Annoying as. No way I was doing it. He kept on being annoying so I hit him too. Sorry Sandy, you aren't that annoying normally. Don't make a habit of it. Anyway, that's why I reckon I might have failed. Sit-u-a-shuns. And I was different every time."

'Seems to me like you might have done OK, Nellie. You don't want to overthink things.' That all sounded typical Nellie to Sandy.

"Nobody ever accused me of overthinking, boy."

Gunny interrupted the conversation. Where did he come from? "Lieutenant, I took the opportunity to have citizenship examinations administered to recruits Nellie and Jane this afternoon."

Nellie and Jane looked at each other and winced.

"It may well have been wiser to wait, or at least to have given them some notice."

That didn't sound good.

"However, they both passed."

This time Sandy was sure that was a smile from Gunny. At least a twitch.

"With your permission, I will now activate their chips."

'Go ahead Gunny.'

"Citizen Recruits, bend your heads forward." Gunny had one of those screwdriver things. One touch each and they were done.

"Jeez Sandy, you are the golden boy."

'Shuddup Nellie.'

Sandy had never been to an airport before, so he didn't know what to expect. He rode there with Corporal Afa and Gunny in the same covered truck they had taken to the Stargate. Through the gates and right up to the airplane. The big airplane. A Dreamliner Corporal Afa had called it. Rode up a platform thing to the door, where the steward showed him to his suite – bedroom, bathroom, combined lounge and dining area. Not big, but pretty comfy. It looked as though there were four suites at the front of the plane.

"The Senator would like a few words with you when you are settled in, Founder." There were stewards up this end of the plane.

'Now's good for me, thanks.'

The Senator's suite was nearer the cockpit.

"Come in Sandy, have a seat. Gunny will be along in a minute. What would you like to drink? Anything to eat?"

Orange juice and a steak roll. That would do Sandy for a midnight snack.

"Well, you've been seventeen for two days now. What do you think of it?"

'Honestly, I haven't had much of a chance to think, Senator. Just watching so far.'

"That will all change soon enough."

There was something Sandy wanted to ask the Senator. Now was as good a time as any.

'Senator, what is the story with Ben? I asked HAL but he said it was your story to tell.'

"Well, we might have a minute or two before Gunny has tucked the troops in and made sure everything is secure to his satisfaction.

The Old Man placed the eleven of us in three different boarding schools. Luke, Red, Bluey, and I went to one. Ben, Jules, Mike and Mark went to another. They were expensive schools, and I guess that Ben, like Mike and Mark came to believe that they were better than other people. In many ways it's hard to come out of an expensive boarding school without that attitude.

When we started college, The Old Man got all of us together and explained our origins. He regarded us as humanity 2.0, a Beta version of humanity, the next step in human evolution. Ben, and he wasn't alone, thought about this, and decided that we were better than the ords, and that their extinction was only a matter of time. It seemed to him a pretty simple application of the principles of natural selection.

He appreciated, as we all did, that there were just too many Alphas for us to announce ourselves. For a while he went along with the old man's strategy of building Uso Dex. However, the pace was too slow for him. He thought that the way to ensure our safety was for us to rule the Alphas. Military conquest was out of the question, at that time. Ben thought the way forward was through politics.

And that was the big division. I followed the Old Man in his belief that we should work on building our knowledge and strength until we could leave this planet. Ben thought that we should use our wealth to rule the Alphas. He thought we would never have to leave. The Alphas would fade away, maybe with a bit of a nudge from us, and the planet would be ours.

We were split. Ben was supported by Jules, Mike and Mark. I was in a group with Luke, Red, David, and Dean. It was 5-4 with Bluey and Dick not really caring either way, so long as nothing got in the way of their research.

The debate went on for a number of years. Uso Dex got bigger, and eventually Jules decided to get rid of us. He set a trap which would have resulted in Luke, Dean and I being killed. We avoided that, although it led to my court martial. I hunted Jules down and killed him.

The only way forward from there was for Ben and his supporters to leave Uso Dex. In the end, Mike and Mark stayed. I entered politics to keep an eye on Ben's activities here, but he left the country. We don't know what he has been doing for the last fifty years."

Sandy had questions, but Gunny Shane came into the lounge.

"Time for take-off Senator. Shall we remain here?"

"Good idea Gunny. We have some things to talk about."

The steward came in, took away their glasses and plates, and checked that their seatbelts were fastened. No-one spoke as the plane taxied to the runway, stood still as the engines raced faster and faster, and then accelerated down the runway. Sandy was pretty sure he felt the plane leave the ground.

"Gunny, that Chinese trap, what do you make of it?"

"As you know Senator, I believe that the Chinese have a population of Choo, maybe of Gooch, and they used us to eliminate their population of obsolete humanzee, or a part of that population. They now know our capabilities in small group engagement. And they have the body of a Gooch which will give them more information."

"They were very wasteful of their humanzee. That's true. So that's why you changed your mind about leaving through the Stargate?"

"Yes, Senator, it is. If there is a population of Gooch, or of Choo, over there we should offer them the opportunity to leave with us."

"So, how many of you are staying?"

"Five."

"Humanzees, chimp-human hybrids without back breeding to human are an obsolete technology. The Chinese are thirty years behind us there. You're right, having the body of a Gooch may jump-start a stalled program. There's something else Gunny. I suspect China may be where we will find Ben."

"Senator?"

"It's only a hunch. The Chinese just aren't the people to want humanzees, straight chimpanzee-human hybrids. They regard humanity as being in three levels. At the top is the ruling class of China. Next are the Chinese as a group. At the bottom is the rest of humanity, whom Chinese regard as infra-humans. For centuries China was closed to the rest of humanity. Racial purity is very important. There is no place in that structure for humanzees. If the Chinese want laborers they have hundreds of millions of peasants.

With Ben though, it's a bit different. We had humanzees when he left Uso Dex. The back breeding with humans and then the artificial breeding of those grandchildren of humanzee who were neither too human nor too chimp had not started. He would have wanted to continue that line of research just to ensure he kept in touch with us. That boy is a chess player. He'd want to be in a position to cover any move we made. It seemed he missed the back breeding with human bit.

In the last week or two, Luke and Red have become convinced that China has developed a racially selective biological weapon, a genocide device. North Korea has killed four Jewish members of the US embassy in Seoul, and has threatened to exterminate the Jews, if South Korea and Japan are not ceded to North Korea. They seem to have released the weapon in New Ziland through a new whooping cough vaccine."

"And you believe that weapon is linked to Uso Dex research before Ben left."

"Yes. I do. It's old research TOM did with the North Vietnamese when everyone thought race was all about specific genes."

'And is that why you are going to New Ziland, Senator?'

"One reason, Sandy. We have the first doses of anti-toxin to deliver to our people in New Ziland. Red has really been quite busy developing it. Red and I are going to attend a meeting to talk about the deaths in vaccinated babies. And, as you know, our Gooch is to be arrested at the request of the FBI."

"If Ben has a position of influence in China that just adds uncertainty."

"Too right, Gunny."

"Invading China and extracting any Choo or Gooch that are there is not going to be simple Senator."

"It is not. We need to know where the Gooch or Choo are, if they exist, first of all. HAL is onto that."

"Lieutenant, it has been another long day for you. I suggest you get some sleep. Tomorrow could be your first taste of combat."

Sandy was kinda annoyed, the way Gunny mothered him. He could look after himself. But, yeah, he was tired so he unbuckled his seat belt and stood up. A steward appeared from nowhere.

"Can I show you to your suite, Founder?"

"See you in the morning Sandy. Perhaps you could have a bite to eat here with me before we land?"

'Yeah, sure. Thanks, Senator.'

Chapter Eleven

In New Ziland, the police came for Adam Gooch at six fifteen in the morning. Any earlier and it would have been too dark for the TV cameras. Any later and they would have missed the breakfast TV shows.

First, the TV crews were escorted to the street and given time to set up.

Then two helicopters, borrowed, with pilots, from the air force, approached the house, one from the north and one from the south.

Black garbed and heavily armed figures began to rappel from the aircraft as two Armed Offender Squad buses raced down the street and skidded to a halt in front of the house.

Four police cars with sirens screaming and lights blazing followed.

The effect was ruined somewhat as Adam Gooch, in a hooded tracksuit, cup in hand, wandered down the road from his early morning coffee run and retrieved the newspaper from his letterbox.

He walked up to the TV presenter, as the officers from the helicopters reached the ground and the armed offenders squad members completed their offensive structure, weapons trained on the house.

"Good morning Pam. What is going on here?"

"Well, you are to be arrested and extradited to the United States."

"I think their plan would work better if I were inside the house. Are you broadcasting live?"

The presenter looked at her cameraman, who looked at someone else who nodded.

"Pam Tree here, coming to you live from the police raid on the house of Mr Adam Gooch, director of security for Uso Dex here in New Ziland, who is wanted by the United States government on charges of bio-terrorism. I am talking to Mr Gooch now."

Behind them black garbed figures charged through the front door of the house. Members of the Armed Offenders Squad fired tear gas grenades through the house windows.

"Mr Gooch, what do you have to say for yourself?"

Adam stood tall, looked at the camera, and said "I am a citizen of Rome."

In the background, viewers got to watch the armed police throw tear-gas through windows, kick down the unlocked front door, shout 'clear' many times, and finally gather round outside the house.

Eventually, one of them realized that Adam was not in the house. He looked puzzled, finally figured it out and walked towards Adam and the reporter, followed by half a dozen others.

"Step away from the hostage Mr Gooch."

Then there were six of them, surrounding the reporter and her cameraman.

"Do you feel threatened, Pam?"

"No, of course not. What did you mean by 'citizen of Rome'?"

Two of the policemen fired their Tasers. They were two or three meters away so perhaps that explains why one of them missed, and hit the reporter who fell to the ground convulsing. The Taser that hit the Gooch had no effect. Adam reached down, pulled the barb from his neck and offered it back to the officer.

"Do you want to try again, officer? Maybe if I moved closer."

"Get on the ground. Hands behind your head."

"No, I don't think I will. Quite happy to accompany you chaps. Your car or mine?"

The reporter continued to jerk about on the ground. The TV cameras were fixed on her.

Adam started walking back toward his front door. A TV cameraman, camera on his shoulder, followed him.

He approached a gaggle of men in black. "Can I help you gentlemen?"

"Get back behind the tape, Sir. No civilians allowed here. We are looking for a dangerous terrorist."

Another officer had followed the TV cameraman. He fired his Taser which hit Adam in the back, without effect.

Adam proceeded up the steps and into his house, with the cameraman.

"Hey, I told you..."

Slowly it dawned on the officers that they would have to start this whole house raid thing again, now that Adam was inside.

Pam Tree had recovered from the Taser strike, and she limped up to the door and inside the house while the police regrouped outside. She saw Adam sitting in his favorite chair, watching the breakfast show on TV.

"Ms Tree. Come in. It's great viewing. Maybe you should phone your office. They seem a little lost."

Back in the studio, there did seem to be a lot of confusion.

"...suggestion now that the whole proceedings have been a promotional gimmick.... Although that Taser hit seemed real enough..."

"I want to go live. Patch us in.."

Her jacket microphone was working.

"Turn your sound off please Mr Gooch. … This is Pam Tree reporting live from the home of Mr Adam Gooch, chief of security for Uso Dex in New Ziland. Last night this station was tipped off by the police that they would be arresting Mr Gooch this morning at the request of US authorities who allege that Mr Gooch is a dangerous bio-terrorist.

What you have seen in the last ten minutes has been real. I don't think the police officers in charge will be getting their good conduct certificates from the FBI this time. The helicopters found the right house, but did not realize that Mr Gooch was out getting his morning coffee when they dropped in. Some idiot tried to Taser Mr Gooch and hit me instead.

At this stage Mr Gooch has not been arrested. He is back inside drinking his coffee and reading his newspaper while forty or so police officers mill around outside."

"Pam, what can you tell us about the charges faced by Mr Gooch?"

"Very little is known at the moment. I am expecting to hear more later in the day when Mr Gooch is due to appear in the Manukau District Court."

I am a citizen of Rome.

HAL picked up the code phrase from the television broadcast. In ancient times, a citizen of Rome had the right to be tried before Caesar, not before a magistrate in the provinces. More recently, the British had understood the phrase to mean that every subject of the British Empire should be protected by that Empire, anywhere in the world, and without regard to local law.

For Citizen Adam Gooch and his family, his use of that phrase, his claim to a basic right of citizenship, directed the full resources of Uso Dex towards him.

"Senator, Lieutenant, Citizen Adam Gooch has requested our help."

HAL patched the Senator into the broadcast from New Ziland and then phoned the managing partner of the leading law firm Uso Dex retained in New Ziland. Five minutes later the Minister of Police had a phone call, in her limousine, from a senior barrister. She was on her way to a breakfast TV interview to discuss the government's plan to increase spending on the police. Even she realized that the agenda had changed. Four lawyers already in at their office piled into a taxi and headed off to Mr Gooch's house with the promise that they would know why before they arrived.

A police dog raced in the front door of Adam's house and bit the cameraman. It was followed by two policemen who tackled the cameraman to the ground, handcuffed him, and dragged him outside. The camera fell to the floor, facing the front door. The televised pictures, from floor level, were dramatic.

A few minutes later, the cameraman limped back inside, with his leg heavily bandaged. Wrong guy, sorry.

This too was shown live on breakfast TV.

Ms Tree was in fine form. In front of a national audience that was increasing by the minute, she laid into the police.

"And don't you even think about firing more tear gas into this house. You idiots have already Tasered me. I don't want to be gassed. Mr Gooch is happy to attend court, so why don't you all just piss off, you puffed up little shits."

Not particularly professional, but she had her reasons.

The police weren't finished. Ms Tree was able to inform Adam that it looked like they were going to rush the house. The cameras, inside the house and outside, captured it all. The preparation, the charge, and then the exit, as policemen were thrown out of windows and doors.

It stopped being funny when shots were heard.

The last policeman landed untidily. Thrown somewhat awkwardly through the lounge window, he turned and folded a bit in the air, like one of those high jumpers.

On TV, viewers see the footage as the police rush Adam, 160kg Adam, in the hallway of his home, and are thrown forward out the other door. Finally there was just one left. Clearly terrified he draws his gun.

"Why don't you just leave officer? My arms are getting tired from throwing you guys out."

The officer is trembling. The name on his overalls is "Monk". He closes his eyes and fires, and fires, and fires, until all nine rounds are gone. Adam walks up to him, picks him up, takes him into the lounge, and throws him out the window. When he turns to face the camera, it is obvious he has been hit four times. Once in the left shoulder, once in the right arm, once in the right thigh, and once in the left side of his stomach.

Ms Tree is incensed, and lets her audience know.

"Unarmed, and prepared to accompany the officers. I even heard him ask, 'your car or mine'. This is a disgrace. Constable Monk is a fool and a coward. If he hadn't been so busy peeing his pants with his eyes closed Mr Gooch would be dead by now."

Chapter Twelve

CC Afa had shaken Sandy awake, gently, as they commenced their descent into Auckland. He had left the reservation at twenty-one thirty Tuesday and was arriving at oh five thirty Thursday. Strange things, the dateline and time-zones. It was only a thirteen hour flight.

He had showered and dressed in the rather classy suit CC Afa had laid out for him to greet immigrations and customs.

The message from HAL came through "Senator, Lieutenant, Citizen Adam Gooch has requested our help."

"Sandy, would you join me please?"

The Senator was in his lounge, with Red.

"Sandy, if you have no objection I will take overall command of the platoon today. You will retrieve Abel Gooch with Abel troop. Bravo troop under Sergeant Max will med-evac Citizen Adam Gooch."

'Nah, I don't mind at all Senator.'

As they landed he had a glass of juice and a bite to eat. Next thing he knew there was a customs and immigration official on the plane. His black Tongan diplomatic passport was handed up by CC Afa, and the officials left. Tongan? Sandy had no idea how he had become a Tongan diplomat.

Two minutes later, Sandy and the Senator were talking with Gunny, Sergeant Max, and Corporals Dave and Afa.

'Sergeant Max I want Citizen Adam Gooch back here, quick as you can. Take your troop. Wait one. HAL, are you there?'

"Good morning Senator. Did you have a pleasant flight?"

'Yes. Thank you for asking. What is happening with Adam?'

"He is currently in his lounge with a TV presenter and her cameraman. He has been shot four times with a Glock pistol. One wound, to his shoulder, affects his combat readiness. There is considerable confusion among the attacking force of police. We have a team of lawyers that have just arrived on site."

"Can you order the police force to maintain a perimeter only, and can you then block further communications to it?"

"I can fake a call to the on-site commander from Commissioner Hedge and can then overload their communications hub with ten million communications per second."

"Do that, please. Sergeant Max, what do you propose?"

"My troop drives to that location. We kill everyone who might be hostile, and return here with Citizen Adam Gooch." Sandy liked the plan.

"That will be plan B. HAL do we have a trauma surgeon that we can call on in this town? If we do, can he make a house call here? We will transport Citizen Adam to the plane where the surgeon can patch him up. He won't be making his court appearance."

"Certainly Senator. If you would like to get Sergeant Max and his men on their way, the surgeon will be here in the mobile field hospital when they return."

"HAL can I speak to the lawyer please?"

"Please hold. I will put you on a conference call with him and those at the house."

"So Sergeant, you are to recover Citizen Adam Gooch from his house. No guns, but Corporal Dave you will take anti-personnel drones with orders to fire upon and kill any person who points a firearm at any of the team. Send recruits Nellie and Jane in. Dismissed"

"Sir."

Corporal Afa looked up from his tablet.

"Senator, Adam Gooch is appearing in courtroom one of the Manukau District Court at ten hundred hours. Ground floor. He is not currently being in police custody. In fact…" and he brought up the live feed from breakfast TV. They were replaying the shooting of Adam by the terrified cop, with the studio announcer providing a summary of the events.

"Your call is ready, Senator."

'Good morning. Who is on the line?'

"Colin Coffers, Queen's Counsel, retained to represent Messrs Adam and Abel Gooch in these proceedings. Am I speaking to the Senator?"

"John Jones, Simon Bell, Matt Grace, and Diane Fort for Mr Gooch. We are outside his house."

"Yes, Mr Coffers you are. One thing at a time. I have sent a team to Mr Gooch's home. They will retrieve him and bring him to me at the airport where he will be seen by a trauma surgeon. He will be treated and you will deal with his court appointment please."

"Jones speaking. That will not be possible. The police are here to arrest him."

"I am sorry if I was not clear Mr Jones. The team I have sent is a combat team. They are armed and expecting to exchange fire. Mr Gooch is coming here. The only uncertainty is the body count at the house. That is for you to control."

"Has Mr Gooch been arrested yet Jones?"

"No Mr Coffers he has not"

"Then you get your butt inside that house right now and make sure he is not arrested. He can come and go as he pleases for so long as the police don't touch him."

"But…"

"No buts. Go now."

"Bell, do we have a copy of the paperwork."

"No Mr Coffers we do not."

"I need that emailed to me right now. I have a court appearance in a few hours. Senator, I will get Mr Gooch out of the house and on the way to your location."

"Thank you Mr Coffers. I have another matter to attend to for the next wee-while. Would you mind dealing with Mr Nelson on my behalf until I can get back to you?"

"Certainly."

"He will meet you at the Courthouse. Could someone be outside for him?"

"Certainly"

"Senator, Founder, we have a problem." Corporal Stan from Charlie troop interrupted.

"What is it Citizen Corporal?"

"There is something amiss at the secure facility where Abel Gooch is being held. It seems like a riot. The local guards have lost control of the wing in which young Mr Gooch is being held."

"Gunny?"

"Senator?"

'No restriction on force. I want that boy out of there. Load up. When can you leave?"

"One minute Senator"

"Very good. CC Afa could you bring recruits Nelson and Jane in please? Oh, and HAL, could I have diplomatic passports for Mr Adam Gooch and his family? No rush, so long as they leave here with Citizen Nelson...Mr Coffers are you still on the line?"

"Yes, Senator I am"

"Sorry about the interruption. But that does bring you up to date about my other matter. By the way, you will find that Mr Adam Gooch bears a diplomatic passport issued by the Kingdom of Tonga. Thank you for your services."

Hang up. "HAL, can you sort the entry records out for me?"

"As we speak, Senator."

"Thanks, I owe you one."

"You owe me four thousand eight hundred and thirty seven Senator. But your credit is good around here."

"Ahh, Sandy your recruits are here."

'Gidday. Sightseeing is off I'm sorry.'

"Wassup Sandy?"

'The Senator has a job for you.'

"Him, is he the Senator?"

'Yes, Nellie, he is the Senator.'

"OK. Gidday Senator."

"Good morning Citizens. Have a look at the news broadcast. You two are going to be point on a mission to Manukau District Court. You are going in as lawyers. Mr Coffers is our lead counsel. He is waiting for your call. Give him the passports for Mr Gooch and his family. They will be ready before you leave. Have something to eat before you go. We are here to rescue two of our citizens, Adam Gooch and his son Abel. If they appear in Court this morning something will have gone badly wrong. However, I need eyes there just in case we have to extract either or both of them from custody. Do not, I say again, do not attempt an extraction without checking with me first. Is that understood?"

"Understood, Senator."

"What's a Court? And what's a lawyer? Do I get a rifle? Can I shoot them?"

Busy, busy, busy. Sandy walked to the back of the plane, and out, down the steps. They were parked inside a large hangar. Door closed. Abel troop had debussed and were loading up a van. Next to the van was a decent sized car, black.

'How many vehicles do we have Gunny?'

"The Senator is taking the limo, but the sedan is here for you. The rest of the troop will travel in the van"

'That's fine. CC Afa is with me. I'll need a driver. Gooch. Armed. How many drones?'

"I'll be escorting you, Sir. Corporal Afa will drive. Four drones. All surveillance anti-personnel. Two have bullets, two missiles."

'OK. We're gone. The rest of the troop can follow.'

Golly, it was already eight o'clock.

There was a lot of information for Sandy to get his head around on the short trip to the secure facility.

The display showed an overhead map of the facility and a floor plan. CC Afa was able to tap into the closed circuit TV feed as well as the radio communications between staff on site.

The drones arrived on station within a few minutes. Their immediate job was to locate Abel using the signal from his biochip. There. In D block. He had barricaded himself into a cell, and there was a group of perhaps twenty targets outside trying to start a fire.

The radio chatter was not reassuring.

"D block sealed off Warden. They are rioting in there. It seems that inmate Gooch is the target."

"Standard protocol. Do not attempt to rescue the inmate at this time. The cavalry is on the way."

At least that limited the hostiles to a group of thugs, until the cavalry, whatever that was, showed up.

'Gunny, how far out is the rest of the troop?'

"Five minutes, founder."

'We will make the rescue ourselves. The troop will cover our exit.'

"Sir. Thirty seconds out."

'CC Afa, I want the drones to remove the exterior wall of D block and to kill every inmate able to pose any threat to Abel. I want to park this vehicle outside the wall, walk inside, and walk out with Abel.' Oh yeah, Sandy had seen lots of movies. He knew how this was done.

"Understood it is, Founder. Kill every inmate able to pose any threat to Abel?"

'Kill them all. Let God sort 'em out.' He'd always wanted to use that line. It was one of his favorites. Anyway, none of that China raid stuff where the drones let someone be captured was going to happen here.

Five seconds before they came to it, the fence in front of them was demolished by an explosion. The drones were onto it.

'Gunny, with me. CC stay here.'

Gunny Shane and Sandy exited the vehicle and walked toward the exterior wall of D block. They were thirty meters from the wall when it was hit by a rocket. The explosion left a large hole through which Gunny and Sandy walked side by side.

Inside, the two bullet drones had killed a number of young hoods. Others were looking up, trying to identify the source of the bullets, and were dying where they stood.

Gunny and Sandy walked in, side by side, and directly to Abel's door.

"Abel Gooch. I am Citizen Master Gunnery Sergeant Shane Gooch of Uso Dex. Your father has requested that we retrieve you. Come out and with us please."

There was some noise behind the cell door, and then Abel appeared, with a towel around his waist. He leaned on the door.

"Gidday. Pleased to see you. I think I've been cut." He turned to show two stab wounds to his back, one on his right side, the other lower down on his left. Blood all over his back, and the towel was red behind.

Gunny Shane moved forward, lifted Abel over his shoulder and began walking out the way they had come, stepping over and around several bodies.

He was still a few meters from the hole in the wall, when Sandy following him, walking backwards so as to keep the hoods in view saw men in black, eight of them, come through the door to the block. These were combat soldiers. They split, took cover.

'Gunny, soldiers to our rear.'

"More commandos is coming round the side of the building." Corporal Afa over the radio.

'Have the drones take them out. Bring the car to us Corporal. Put Abel down Gunny. It'll be faster if we both support one shoulder. Abel you gotta run man…How far out is the rest of the troop, Corporal...and how did those men in black get here?'

"Ninety seconds lieutenant. Recommend you is taking cover. The attacking forces is being in enfilade very soon."

'Negative. We're leaving and the rest of the troop is to prevent any pursuit from this location.'

"Understood you is. One bullet drone is exiting the building. The other is engaging the commandos in there, as they is attempting to move forward. One missile drone has fired at the group coming round the side of the building. The second bullet drone will engage that group as it emerges from cover. The second missile drone is searching for their vehicle and will destroy it when found."

'Destroy any vehicle capable of transporting the troop of commandos. Not just the one that got them here.' Yep, Sandy had seen lots of movies. He knew how things happened.

"Understood you is."

They met the sedan fifty meters from the wall of D-block. Afa placed the vehicle between then and the attacking force. Sandy pushed Abel into the back seat and followed him in. Gunny sat up front with Afa. They passed the rest of the troop in their van one hundred meters from the jail.

HAL's voice came over the net.

"Founder, with your permission, once the site is secure, I want the dead commandos fingerprinted and photographed and pictures of their dog tags too."

'Agreed. CC?'

"In position now Lieutenant. Advancing. Photography by missile drone...Missile drone is destroying a United States military helicopter, Lieutenant."

'Have the van follow us back to the airport Corporal. One kilometer separation. Monitor all radio chatter please CC; military, police, prison, and media.'

"CC? Is you talking to me?"

'Yep, that's you Citizen Corporal Afa.'

Sergeant Max and his troop had it easy. They did not stop at the barricades set up to block off Adam's street. The police officer manning them was wise enough to jump aside as the truck rolled through.

Two officers were run over as the truck, horn blaring, drove up onto Adam's front lawn.

Sergeant Max's six soldiers debussed and strode towards Adam's front door. Policemen moved aside, not knowing what was happening, and within thirty seconds Adam was in the van and gone. Mrs Gooch was not at home. She was at her parents'.

Ms Tree and her cameraman were left, standing outside the house, with Jones, the lawyer.

The Senator had left by the time Sandy arrived back at the airport. He traveled to the city, with Red, in a spacious black limousine with the second Gooch, Marty, from Bravo troop, imposing as hell in a black suit, sunglasses and an earpiece, upfront with the driver.

Sandy hadn't noticed the security guard at the gate on the way out. He'd been too busy studying maps and things. He noticed him now. The barrier arm stayed down and the guard moved toward the driver's window, CC Afa's window. CC Afa didn't slow. The barrier arm lifted, and they were through. That was weird.

Back in the hangar there was a lot going on. A lot. A tent, yep it was a tent, was inflating over in one corner. CC Afa drove that way. Sandy was a bit worried about Abel. It looked like a lot of blood. Sandy had taken off his jacket, and his shirt. He knew about applying pressure, but it wasn't that easy, not on someone's back when they were sitting up. He'd tried wiping away the blood, but that hadn't really worked. He could see one wound was kind of spurting. Kind of. Every second or so, like a ripple of blood would overflow out of the cut. He wadded his shirt up and had Abel hold it in place. There was another wound. It was bigger and blood was just leaking out of it. The kidney was under there someplace. That's where Sandy put his jacket. No way Abel could get his hand round to apply pressure there, so Sandy was pressing on the jacket.

The car stopped. Gunny was out and around to Abel's door. Two seconds and Abel was out and onto a trolley.

Sandy got out. Citizen Sergeant Harley was coming over to him. Nellie and Jane were running across. But, the man in charge was a tall, lean Alpha, standing beside a medical gurney. A citizen major according to the blue holographic insignia Sandy could see above his shoulders.

"Lie him here on his front thank you soldier... Medic, I want vitals. I have the trauma pack. Inserting 14 gauge line into antecubital fossa. Done. Opening saline pack. Using contents to wash the back. Two wounds of note. One superficial. Small bleeder. Clamped in passing. The other wound is over the left kidney. Will need to be explored in theatre. Triage category delayed. Twenty minutes theatre time required. What are those vitals?"

"Patient conscious. BP one ten over seventy, pulse fifty-two. Pupils equal and reactive."

"Thank you... Soldier, my name is Major Bolton. I am a trauma surgeon. You have a stab wound to your back that I need to have a look at in theatre, and another small wound that needs a stitch or two. There is another patient inbound, but I think I'll have a look at you now... Let's move. What about you son, is that your blood?" Mr Bolton was talking to Sandy. What blood? Sandy shook his head.

And they were gone. Into the tent. Citizen Sergeant Harley was there, standing at attention. Nellie and Jane were there, not standing at attention.

"How come you lost your suit? That your blood? You shoot anybody? We gotta get going Jane. There's shooting and stuff out there."

CS Harley explained that the tent Sandy had seen was a mobile field hospital, normally stored in a container in the hangar. Bravo troop had recovered Mr Gooch and was ten minutes out.

Nellie and Jane were off, to Court. Sandy wasn't sure why. All they had left to do now was deliver those passports. Both Adam and Abel Gooch were going to be here. But, orders were orders. He went back into the plane, had a shower, and put a uniform on. He liked his uniform, especially the pip which said he was a lieutenant.

There wasn't a lot to do. Mr Adam Gooch arrived, and got taken into the hospital tent. The Senator was still at his meeting.

HAL asked if he wanted to look in on the Manukau District Court video. Yep.

Chapter Thirteen

Nellie and Jane were driven to the Manukau District Court by Private First Class Lopa of Charlie troop. The journey from the airport was slow, and they arrived outside the building shortly before ten hundred hours. PFC Lopa decided to park the car at a shopping center across the road.

Jane had looked it up, and was trying to explain courts and lawyers to Nellie. He was not impressed.

"You mean, it takes months or years to decide if some dude hit another one?"

"Yes."

"What? They aint got no cameras?"

"Nah, not like us."

"And peeps don't speak for themselves. That's what lawyers do?"

"Yes."

"And if you do break the rules you get locked in jail and are useless for years?"

"Yes."

"That's dumb. They're idiots. This war thing should be easy."

There was a lawyer waiting for them at the entrance to the Court. Nellie handed her the passports, and she escorted them through the security scans.

"Mr Coffers is waiting for you in an interview room outside courtroom four."

Jane felt like her head was on a swivel. She had thought of a Court as something like a library, quiet and dignified, but this was nothing like that. It was a miserable place. Dirty. Crowded. There were police, in uniform. There were lawyers, in suits and looking busily superior. There were people, lots of people. Many with children. Some looked angry. Most just looked confused and beaten. The interview room was small, and Mr Coffers seemed stressed.

Nellie introduced them.

"Well met Mr Nelson. That anti-ageing drug must be very effective. You barely look twenty….Thank you for the passports. They will be helpful. ….Mr Adam Gooch is not at court. The Senator has been kind enough to set up a live video feed to the operating theatre where he is currently undergoing surgery. I see that Mr Abel Gooch was also to appear here this morning. However it appears he is no longer in custody. That will be a problem with this judge… his honor, Anders Willnow… There is one matter to be heard before ours. A sentencing….I have two lawyers holding aisle seats for you in the courtroom. If you would excuse me, I have one or two details to attend to before the court opens."

They were in courtroom one. The lawyer showed them the seats being saved for them, and they sat down.

"What you think?"

"Our boys aren't here. We should learn what we can about security all the same." Nellie didn't really want to know what she thought. He wasn't interested in the despair all around them. The despair that made Jane just want to pick up a gun and open fire. The more of these people she shot, the greater the gain in average ord happiness. Nellie was only interested in physical things. Right now, how would they rescue the Gooch and his son from here if it came to that?

"Yeah. Lots of glass windows. Just grab him and run. Easy."

A door opened behind the bench. A lady came in, and announced "All stand for his honor, District Court Judge Anders Willnow."

The judge entered, robes flowing around him. He stood behind the bench, nodded his head at the lawyers in front of him, said, "Be seated", and sat down himself.

The man seated immediately below the bench rose. "The Police versus Shane Boggs to be followed by The Queen versus Adam Gooch."

A door in the side wall at the front of the court opened, and a small man in an ill-fitting grey suit was pushed towards the dock where he stood, hands behind his back.

A lawyer stood, "Mr Fine for the police Sir."

Another lawyer stood, "Ms South for the prisoner Sir."

It seemed that Boggs had been in a car driven by his wife when they had encountered a police stop, checking drivers for alcohol. His wife had failed the initial in-car screening and was required to enter the "booze bus". Boggs had interfered with this, and had finished up attempting to head butt a constable. He had made contact with the officer's shoulder and been charged with assaulting a police constable. The facts were not in dispute, and Boggs appeared today for sentence.

Mr Fine felt that a sentence of community service was called for.

Ms South agreed, but said that Boggs was employed and able to pay a fine, and so perhaps his community service could be somewhat shorter than the three hundred hours sought by Mr Fine.

At this point Mr Coffers, followed by four other lawyers entered the courtroom. He stood behind the bar until one row was cleared for him.

Judge Willnow scowled, but said nothing. He looked down at some papers in front of him. Looked up, and said to Boggs.

"Mr Boggs, please stand."

Boggs was already standing.

"Mr Boggs you have pleaded guilty to one charge of assaulting a police officer. I see that you have previously appeared before this Court. Twenty one years ago you were sentenced to two years imprisonment for selling marijuana. At that time you were a member of a motorcycle gang. I sentence you today to one week in jail."

Why on the New World would the judge do that? Maybe Nellie was right and this war would be easy. Maybe not.

Ms South was up on her feet immediately.

"Your honor, I apply for bail pending appeal."

"Application dismissed. Officer, take the prisoner away. Next matter."

Once again the suited man in front of the bench rose.

"The Queen versus Adam Gooch, followed by the Queen versus Abel Gooch."

"Fine for the Queen Sir"

"Coffers for Mr Gooch Sir"

"Your honor, I have received applications from TV One and TV3 to record these proceedings."

"Do you have any objection Mr Coffers?"

"No Sir"

"The proceedings may be recorded by TV One and TV3"

"Thank you, your honor. .."

Mr Fine was interrupted by Mr Coffers rising to his feet.

"Mr Coffers, I don't know how you do things in Wellington, but up here it is discourteous to come to your feet while the Crown is making its introductory comments."

"Thank you, your honor. But there are a couple of preliminary issues."

"Have you raised them with the Crown Mr Coffers."

"I am doing so now your honor."

"This is a simple matter. Extradition of a terrorist. What possible preliminary matters can there be?"

"Alleged terrorist, your honor. It is my contention that this Court does not have jurisdiction. The very foundation of the Crown case is that, under American law, my client is, himself, a non-human animal weapon of mass destruction. This Court's jurisdiction in extradition does not extend to non-human animals."

"That's an argument for another day. Your second matter?"

"Mr Gooch bears a diplomatic passport issued by the Kingdom of Tonga. The Crown has made no request that diplomatic immunity be waived, and therefore there is no legal basis on which Mr Gooch can be detained, much less held in custody."

"Well, where is Mr Gooch? Why is he not in the dock?"

"Your honor, the police attempted to arrest Mr Gooch at his home this morning but he resisted and was taken to the airport by armed employees of Uso Dex."

"Is this true Mr Coffers?"

"It is true that Mr Gooch has not been arrested your honor."

"Have you received a copy of the arrest warrant Mr Coffers?"

"I have your honor, just over an hour ago."

"Well then your client has been served. Why isn't he here?"

"He is currently in surgery your Honor. He was shot four times by the police."

"You will forgive my skepticism Mr Coffers. Do you have any evidence of this?"

"I have footage of the shooting, and have a video-link to the operating theatre, Sir."

"I am not interested in the footage. Get the surgeon on the line then Mr Coffers."

There was a delay while one of the lawyers talked to the court staff. A cable was run from a laptop to a large flat screen in the courtroom, and within a few seconds everybody in the Court could see inside an operating theatre, where a surgeon was stitching up an incision to the stomach of a large man.

"Mr Bolton, Colin Coffers QC here. I am in the District Court at Manukau. His honor Judge Anders Willnow would like a word with you."

The surgeon looked up and into the camera.

"I have my hands full here Coffers. Make it quick."

"Mr Bolton I am District Court Judge Anders Willnow. Can you confirm that the patient you are operating on is Mr Adam Gooch."

"I have no idea who he is. Look at his face and decide for yourself." That was sensible. The doc had never met the Gooch before today. He hadn't arrived at the airport by the time she and Nellie had left to come here. How could the surgeon confirm that the patient was Adam Gooch?

"You will not speak to me like that in my courtroom."

"I am not in your courtroom. You are in my operating theatre. Now do you have any questions that I can answer? I have a shoulder to save here after I have closed the abdomen and am not particularly interested in your legal games."

"What are your patient's injuries?"

"He has four bullet wounds. One nicked his spleen and resulted in internal bleeding. I have removed his spleen. He requires a blood transfusion but laboratory matching is not complete. He has soft tissue damage to his right arm and right thigh which I shall attend to next. I have not explored his shoulder wound fully, but the joint has been penetrated and reconstruction may be required."

"When can I speak to him?"

"Tomorrow."

"That is not satisfactory."

"It is what it is. I will be operating for, perhaps, another six hours. The patient will not recover from the effects of the anesthetic for a further twelve hours after that, and he will be confined to bed for 48 hours following surgery."

Mr Fine spoke, "Is your patient human Mr Bolton?"

"The anatomy is somewhat irregular, but within the range of human."

"Is your patient human or is your patient an ape?"

"Humans are apes you fool, and I'm a surgeon not a taxonomist."

"Where are you Mr Bolton?"

"In a hangar at the airport."

"You seem to be in an operating theatre Mr Bolton."

"A mobile field hospital, Judge."

Judge Willnow looked away from the screen. "Counsel, there is a warrant for the arrest of Mr Gooch. That cannot be executed at the moment. I am prepared to have a sitting of this Court at Mr Gooch's hospital bedside two pm tomorrow. Are you available?'

Both lawyers were. Mr Fine stood.

"Your honor the defendant is at the airport. He is clearly a flight risk."

"What do you suggest Mr Fine?"

"That this Court remands him in custody."

"He has not been arrested. I can't remand him anywhere. In any case the surgeon says he must be in hospital at least until the time I have allocated for the hearing tomorrow."

"Then he should be under guard."

"I cannot order the police to do that. It is an operational matter for them. Next case please Mr Registrar"

"The Queen versus Mr Abel Gooch."

Once again Mr Fine stood, and informed the Court he was acting for the Crown. Mr Coffers stood for Abel. Mr Fine spoke.

"Mr Abel Gooch is not in Court this morning your Honor. It seems that, in the early hours of this morning, there was an inmate riot in the facility where he is being held and no prisoner transfers to Court were possible. The picture at present is very confused. There appears to have been an explosion at the facility and firearms have been discharged. TV3 is showing footage of the scene which appears to show dead American servicemen and a burning American military helicopter at the site. There is considerable wreckage and it is unknown whether Mr Abel Gooch is injured, dead, or even still held at the facility."

"Mr Fine, are you telling me that American armed forces have attempted to remove, indeed may have removed, Mr Abel Gooch from custody?"

"That seems to be one possibility your honor."

"I will stand this matter down until two pm today at which time I expect better information from you Mr Fine. Do you have any objection to that Mr Coffers?"

"No Sir, I do not."

"Very well, this matter is stood down and will be called again at two o'clock."

Jane had a lot to think about as she left the court. It was the first time she had observed ords in the wild, outside of the reservation. They were not impressive. She had thought, for years, until a few days ago, that the war with the ords would be a desperate and quick thing where the job of the army would be to hold off the ords for as long as they could so that as many citizens, Choo, and Gooch, as possible made it off the planet before the army was overwhelmed and all the soldiers, like Nellie, Sandy, and her, were killed. Kind of like that movie '300'.

When she'd heard the Senator's first speech, she'd expected that she only had a few weeks to live. 1RR would be at the sharp end of any war, and its soldiers wouldn't live for long. She'd worried about how she'd cope if Nellie was killed first. That would be worse than dying herself.

Then the Senator had talked about building a second Stargate to a universe created for humans to colonize. Today, Jane believed, for the first time that perhaps Uso Dex might survive. She understood a bit better the things she'd read in *The Prince* and *The Art of War* about dealing with numerically superior forces. If your enemy has superior strength, divide him or evade him. The supreme art of war is to subdue the enemy without fighting. It is better to be feared than loved.

Suddenly Jane realized that the Senator had been planning and fighting this war for the last fifty years or more. Maybe there was a better planner, or a better fighter, but if so that person wasn't an ord.

She leaned over and kissed Nellie.

"Focus girl. We on a mission, and it's not over till we back on the plane. Soon."

Chapter Fourteen

The Senator didn't look that happy when he arrived back from his meeting. Sandy asked him how it went.

"Pretty much as I expected. The people here think the vaccine batch is faulty, that it lowers immunity so that recipients are vulnerable to another illness and that is what is killing them. That's not what is going on. Here, let me show you this."

A typewritten note appeared on the screen in the Senator's lounge.

"Four American staff in the Seoul embassy have died in the last few days. The dead are Jews, and the first to die had been handed a note by the North Koreans. Let's have a look at the note."

Sandy hadn't seen the note before. It made no sense at all.

THE KILLERS OF FEVASTIN SHALL DIE

THE LAND OF DONKEY SHALL BE CLEANSED

THE HOURIS WILL BE NO MORE

REUNIFICATION

RETURN JAPAN TO KOREA

OR THE JEWISH SOLUTION WILL BRING PEACE TO PALESTINE

"The second half of the note is quite clear. It is a simple piece of blackmail. North Korea threatens to kill the world's Jews if it does not get both South Korea and Japan. And North Korea has demonstrated its ability to kill Jews. The first half of the note makes more sense is the English is improved"

And on the screen, this appeared

THE KILLERS OF FEATHERSTON SHALL DIE

THE LAND OF DON KEY SHALL BE CLEANSED

THE HORIS SHALL BE NO MORE

"They say, Sandy, that revenge is a dish best served cold. Many years ago Japanese and Korean prisoners were massacred by soldier guards at the Featherston Prisoner of War Camp in this country. New Ziland has always treated this as some kind of accident, as though a group of men armed with rifles could unintentionally send co-ordinated fire into unarmed prisoners. Well, as you can see, North Korea does not see it that way and they blame Maori for the massacre. They might be crazy, but even crazy people have opinions.

Don Key is the prime minister of New Ziland.

I think that a race-specific biological weapon of mass destruction is being released into this country. It is being released through a vaccine, but if I were in charge, I would use more than one delivery vector. As soon as we got a sample of the vaccine we recognized the weapon. It's something TOM developed when he was in Vietnam years and years ago. The problem with it, and it is a big one, is that the race targeting is unstable. We believe that the deaths will spread from the Maori to mixed race Maori, and then to other racial groups. There have only been a hundred and something deaths so far, but that will change. We expect hundreds of new cases will be reported today and over a thousand will have died by the weekend."

That didn't sound good.

"But, it's worse than that, Sandy. The research could only have got from Vietnam to North Korea through China. I think China intends to release this weapon against America. War is imminent. HAL is not convinced. He's fixed on the idea that America is China's biggest trading partner. But Germany's biggest trading partners before World War One were Russia, the United Kingdom, and America. Same in World War Two. The biggest trading partners were the first to be attacked."

Not good at all, if you were American. But Uso-Dex had an anti-toxin.

Nellie and Jane arrived back from Court. Nellie was not happy. He thought it had been a waste of time, but there was food on the plane, so he was allgood pretty quickly. Jane, well Jane seemed far too happy.

A Dr Pink arrived. The Senator had invited him over for lunch. And there was that reporter lady on the phone about the rescue of Abel. Sandy had left fourteen dead American servicemen, and twenty-two dead inmates, all aged under seventeen behind. She reckoned that was a lot of lives lost to rescue one boy.

"We only count one, one of our people saved."

Dr Pink had been the only person at the meeting who agreed with the Senator and Red. The Senator wanted to offer him a job. Apparently Uso Dex was setting up a big medical research facility in Australia and wanted Dr Pink to be its head.

"Umm, I don't know.. yeah, sure.. never going to get a better offer, am I? But do you mind if I ask a couple of questions?"

"Ask away."

"Your anti-ageing treatment. Why isn't that available to everyone?"

"The standard fee for our anti-ageing treatment is ten million dollars per patient per year, and Uso Dex has over twelve thousand full fee paying clients who are not getting any older. Costs of production and distribution are one percent of that amount. One hundred and ten billion plus is our annual take from this product. Equally important, these clients are powerful and supportive. The profit from all our other medical products is about half of this amount. That's a lot of profit to give away." Dr Pink did not look impressed. "And our program is untested and unproven. It may not be safe."

"If the federal government paid for the testing...?"

"There is strong opposition within the scientific community to spending federal funds on alternative approaches such as ours.

Even if testing were approved, and even if our program were shown to be safe, and even if we gifted the relevant intellectual property to the nation, at the ten thousand dollars per person per year generic price that has been suggested the country could not afford it. There is disagreement as to whether the country should pay two trillion dollars per year to treat two hundred million people. But if the program worked and if people stopped ageing, what would the country do with them? Everyone wants to live forever but no-one wants everyone to live forever."

Dr Pink had nothing else to say. The Senator escorted him off the plane, and to a waiting taxi. Time to leave. Sandy followed the Senator across to a tent, the mobile field hospital. Once inside, they had to stand in what looked a little like an airlock.

"The operating theatre and recovery room are at positive pressure compared to the rest of the hangar so that bugs can't be blown in."

That seemed like a good idea to Sandy. The Senator pushed some buttons on a monitor on the wall, and they saw Mr Bolton, still in theatre scrubs, disconnecting various machines from Adam Gooch.

"Mr Bolton. Wheels up in twenty."

Mr Bolton looked up.

"Ah, Senator. This patient can be moved. The shoulder is stable but not yet repaired. I can do that at your place."

"Are you prepared to travel with us?"

"If you can provide me with clothes and toiletries. I don't like leaving a job half done."

"It may be some time before we can return you here."

"I understand that. Get some orderlies in here will you?"

"HAL, can you get us loaded up? I would like to be in the air as soon as possible."

"Senator, air traffic control is refusing us clearance to take off."

"I don't have time for this nonsense. Which runway is safest for a take-off without air traffic clearance?"

"Runway seven."

"Inform the pilots that we will be taking off from runway seven. Radio silence till we are taxiing."

It was fifteen minutes, and he was back in the forward lounge with the Senator, Red, and Gunny, seatbelt on, before he felt their plane begin to move.

"Inform air traffic control that this flight is taking off from runway seven."

"Permission denied, Senator."

"Tell them I was not asking for permission. Inform all other flights of our plans."

"There is a firetruck and several airport security vehicles racing to runway seven, Senator. I believe they mean to park on the runway."

"Too many movies. They watch too many movies. HAL, do we have enough time to launch missiles?'

"Yes, Senator. Targets locked."

"Fire."

Sandy saw the missiles flying from, not from under the wing, it looked like they were coming from under the plane. Direct hits on all three vehicles.

A few minutes later they were in the air.

"HAL, are we taking the long way home?"

"Yes Senator. Across to South America and then up."

"Well, Sandy, how was your day?"

How was his day? Sandy really hadn't thought about it that much. Got on a plane to New Ziland. Broke a guy out of prison. Waited round the airport. On the way home now.

'Not bad, Senator. Reckon I might go and check on Abel.' Convos with old people weren't much fun. No point getting into one.

Directly behind the suites was a pretty big, maybe eight meters long area. It had been a lounge a few hours ago. Now it was a hospital, with two beds. Adam Gooch was sleeping in one. Abel was sitting up watching a movie in the other. He had a drip in one arm, and one side was heavily bandaged, with a tube coming through the dressing.

Sandy hadn't realized how big this boy was. Mind you, his father was a Gooch.

'Hi. I'm Sandy.' There was a chair by the bed and Sandy sat in it. 'Just wondered how you were doing?'

"Good. You're one of the guys that rescued me. Thanks."

'Yeah, didn't realize you were so big, or I would have let Gunny carry you all the way.'

"I've always been big. Where did you guys come from?"

'We're from Uso Dex. The police tried to arrest your father this morning. He asked us to get him out of there.'

And then they were talking. It turned out that Abel was fifteen, nearly sixteen. He told Sandy about how he was stopped by the police. How they had found the meth in his car. Sandy told him they knew it had been planted.

"Yeah, I know that. Pleased you guys do too."

He'd got into a bit of a fight at the youth facility yesterday. Was in the yard by himself and the guards had let four other guys in. Bloods. Brown boys with red bandanas.

"It was pretty obvious they wanted to fight. And I was just pissed off. So we fought. The big one had a go at me first, but I just picked him up and threw him into the wall. Heard the cracks. He didn't get up. One of them pulled a knife but he was a dumbass, tried to poke me with it. So I just grabbed his wrist, bent it pretty much all the way forward, bone came through the skin, then I just swung his arm so he stabbed himself in the chest. The last two rushed me, but I broke the elbow of one and the other backed off. He didn't want to fight. Kept saying "It's allgoods. Allgoods eh. Wanna smoke? I can get us some smokes." The guards came back about five minutes later. Made quite a bit of fuss. Asked me, what happened? I just pointed to the cameras. A couple pulled their batons out. I told them where I'd stick their batons, and they opened the gates so I could walk back to my cell.

This morning, they opened my cell, told me to shower. When I was in the shower a whole lot of punks rushed me. Must have been about twenty of them. Had a bit of trouble getting back to my cell. They were trying to set fire to it when you turned up."

'Pretty exciting. You fight much.'

"Nah, that was the first time in ages, since I was about ten. Everyone at school knows I'm real strong."

'You play any sports?'

"Not allowed. Dad says I'm too strong and my temper is too bad. He's right. I watch a bit of league, and I'd kill half the refs."

Sounded like Nellie's kind of guy.

'Hey, you tired, or you want to meet some people?'

"I gotta stay here. Got some stitches, and gave some blood so Dad could have a transfusion."

'They shouldn't be far away. I'll go see.'

And there they were, sitting together. Sandy counted. There were six seats to a row, three either side of the aisle, so ninety seats all up. Most were empty.

The doctor was in the front row. Sandy beckoned to Nellie and Jane. They unbuckled and came to him. Corporal Afa looked up, and then back to his tablet.

'Come, I got someone for you to meet.'

They had to steal a seat from Mr Gooch's bed, but he was still asleep.

'This is Abel. He's the guy we broke out of jail today.'

"Better day than we had. We had to sit in Court. Hey, you were supposed to be there."

"Got any food up here Sandy?"

"Was I? Nobody told me."

Sandy reckoned he knew what that felt like. A steward appeared, pushing a trolley.

"What would you like to eat, Founder?"

HAL hears everything. That could get to be annoying.

A nurse appeared. She poked a thermometer in Abel's ear, took his pulse and blood pressure and said Abel could eat and drink whatever he liked. They had a good feed. Nellie on the steak and fries. Abel had the fish and stir-fry, like Sandy and Jane. Nellie and Abel got talking about rugby league. They were both fans. It was probably about the only sport you could watch on monitors in the reservation. Nellie supported the Roosters. Abel was a Souths fan.

"Hey, Sandy you know what?"

'Nah, what Nellie?'

"You know Jane is going to be a flyboy, eh?"

'Yeah, I heard.' Sandy reckoned Nellie should have worked out that Jane was a girl by now, but, not his business.

"We should have Abel in our troop."

'Ya reckon?'

"Yeah. You know how Gunny was saying Jane and I have to knock on doors, talk to ords before we shoot them, stuff like that?"

'Yeah.' Sandy didn't know, but it was easier to agree.

"Well I don't know crap about ords. But Abel has lived there forever. He could do the talking and when he's done I'll shoot 'em up. Anyways, we're Abel troop, and he's Abel. Where else he gonna go?"

"What's an ord?"

"Them. Not us."

"How do you know I'm not an ord?"

"Your dad. He's a Gooch. You're not an ord. You wanna join the army?"

"Hadn't really thought about it. I'm still getting used to being a convict, on the run."

"Dodge that. Sandy can set it up. Can't you?"

'Dunno. Maybe. Let's get back home first.'

"Yeah. I reckon I got training again tonight. When someone tells me what day it is. Hey where's that tube go?"

Nellie had spotted the clear plastic tube that came from under the large white dressing on Abel's side. He leaned forward for a better look.

"Inside."

"Yeah I guessed that. You gotta big hole in your side? That why you're leaking? I dunno if you can be in the army if you gotta big leaky hole in your side."

"Nah, it wasn't that big. Just deep. The guy who sewed it up said the knife might have cut my kidney. If blood drains out, I might need another operation."

"Cool. Let's see." Nellie reached out and picked the tube up. It was attached to a clear plastic bag. The bag was empty. "Nah. Nothing."

Nellie seemed a bit disappointed, but he came back. "Hey do you know what's going on? With the world, and the Senator, and the Stargate, and the robots, and the Gooch, and the Choo? All that stuff?"

"I've been in jail man. We don't get the newspaper in jail."

"Newspaper. What's a newspaper? Anyway, can we show him Sandy?"

"I can feed it through the screen up there," and Jane pulled a tablet out. This time it almost made sense to Sandy.

Uso Dex had created Gooch and Choo, and now ILFs. These would be destroyed on sight by the ords, or a bounty paid for their capture dead or alive. The Twelve had decided that the best option was to abandon this planet. The Stargate couldn't be kept secret, and so the Senator had made his announcements.

"Hey, but my father's a Gooch."

"Yes, son, I am." Mr Gooch had woken up.

"So you're what, a mixture of gorilla and human?"

Sandy knew the answer to this one. 'Initially a chimpanzee human hybrid, then bred to a gorilla. Two generations bred with human. Two Gooch-Gooch matings since. That's your father. Is your mother human?'

"My mother is Jewish."

"You better join the army then, boy." Nellie's contribution.

"What? Why?" Abel was getting angry.

"You've got chimpanzee and gorilla genes. They'll kill you on sight and get paid a million bucks for it. You're a Beta, like me, like Jane, like Sandy. They're at war with us. Dunno why, but we're looking forward to it. And you've got Jewish genes, so the North Koreans have released this virus thing to kill your ass."

"What are you on about?"

"Let me finish." And Jane showed the tape of Mr Gooch's attempted arrest, of the rescue of Abel, and of the Senator discussing the message from North Korea.

"Does mum know?"

"She heard the Senator's broadcasts, and asked me whether I was a Gooch, like the Senator was talking about. When I said she was, she packed her bags and left."

"Shit dad, I'm sorry. But why didn't you tell her? Why didn't you tell me?"

"I never thought it made a difference. Your mother and I were in love. I still love her, very much. I didn't think whether I had this gene or that gene was so very important to her. And look at you. You are a wonderful son. Why should you be treated as a freak? I'm sorry son if I have let you down"

"Nah, it's just a surprise. And now what, eight billion people want to kill me. And those North Koreans want to poison me. Well frig them. I'm a joining the army. I just hope Nellie's stronger than he looks"

"What? Why?"

"If we're going hunting together, I can carry my share. What about you?"

"Don't worry about me, boy. Don't worry about me. You'll see."

Chapter Fifteen

Sandy had been having a good sleep, when HAL woke him up. Or, HAL's voice coming through the speaker by his head woke him up.

"Good morning Founder. The Senator would like you to breakfast with him when you are ready."

Somehow a new uniform had appeared beside his bed. Toilet, shower, get dressed. Back to the Senator's lounge. They were there already, Shane and Red.

"Good morning Sandy."

'I suppose. What time is it?'

"Oh eight hundred hours reservation time, Lieutenant. We have traveled a seldom used route, flying to the tip of South America and then up over Argentina and Brazil. We are now flying over the Gulf of Mexico, about 300 kilometers from our coast."

'Oh, thanks Gunny.' Sandy helped himself to some of the old people's food on the table – pastries and fruit, and poured himself a juice.

'What happened in New Ziland after we left yesterday?'

"Their prime minister, Don Key, refused to comment on Adam or Abel, saying that our footage was obtained illegally. He maintains that his chief science advisor is correct, and there is no coming epidemic. He describes our actions as terrorism."

'Gunny, what do you say about Abel joining Abel troop?'

"I say no, Lieutenant. But that's not important. What do you say?"

'Well, he's lived among the ords all his life. Nellie, Jane, me, we don't know crap about the ords. And Jane will be leaving Abel troop to become a pilot, so there will be a gap.'

"But, you three have spent all your lives preparing to join the army. You are skilled with small weapons. He is not."

'He's in. He can take over those orderly duties for me that Corporal Afa performs. And he can train up as a medic. We don't have a medic.'

"As you wish, Lieutenant."

'Senator, do we have a pilot attached to 1RR?'

"No. When you order an aircraft, a pilot from the pool is allocated to you."

'I don't want that. I want Jane to be our pilot, and to remain with 1RR.'

"It is your unit Sandy. HAL, can we manage that?"

"Yes, Senator. I will get Corporal Afa onto it."

"Go see a steward Sandy. Get a real breakfast."

'Why's that Senator?'

"You're hungry lad. You're mean when you're hungry."

Back in the lounge hospital, Sandy found a steward. Abel was awake. His father was being examined by Mr Bolton, the surgeon.

'Can we have breakfast for four please?'

"Certainly Founder."

The surgeon looked up and turned around.

"Good morning. My name is Bolton. I operated on these two yesterday."

'Hi, I'm Sandy. How long before Abel can be up and about? He's in the army now.'

"I've removed that drainage tube, and changed his dressing. Of course, he can't train until the stitches come out in ten days, and even then the internal wound will take a further two weeks to heal."

'So, he can walk out of here, in a uniform?'

"Yes, he can."

Sandy thanked the surgeon, and went through the curtain. Nellie and Jane were asleep. Nellie had his arm round Jane. Sandy poked him.

'Wake up soldier. Breakfast time.'

"Breakfast. Good. Hey, wake up Jane."

The steward was setting breakfast up in the lounge hospital. Abel was out of bed, wearing only a towel, sitting in a comfy chair by the food.

"What do you want to eat Dad?"

"No, I'm fine thanks."

'Guess what Abel. You're in the army. In our unit. Gunny's a bit worried, but we'll train you up as a medic and on comms. You gotta look after me too.'

"What's that?"

'Corporal Afa will get you up to speed. You sleep OK?'

"Nah, hardly at all. Lots of movies to choose from though. Hey you never told me you were so important."

'What? Nah, not me.'

"Yeah. That corporal, Afa, looked in on me last night. Stayed for a chat. A long chat. Told me heaps. Said he'd get me something to wear. I left New Ziland wearing a towel, no luggage, and I've lost my towel. Someone left this one by my bed."

"Don't believe it man. That Sandy, he's OK, but him a fool half the time. We gotta look out hard for him now he's got the top job or he'll make us look real bad."

'Thanks Nellie.'

"Anytime, boy."

Sandy returned to the Senator's lounge for landing. He wanted to ask a couple of things.

"Well, Sandy, how's it been, your first mission in command?"

'Pretty good Senator. I didn't have to do much. Most of the time Gunny and Corporal Afa have done the thinking for me... What's going to happen to Adam Gooch now?'

It wasn't a frown, but Gunny didn't seem too pleased at the mention of Adam's name.

"Gunny, what do you think?"

"Citizen Adam Gooch has all the rights of any Uso Dex citizen. However, he will not be allowed to live in the New World. His case was considered some time ago, and the Gooch accept his decision, made seventeen years ago, to attempt to assimilate with the Alphas. His way of life is not ours. It may be that the Senator has a role for him in diplomacy. We do not."

"Does that answer your question Sandy?"

'Yeh, I suppose so.' It sounded pretty harsh actually. 'There's something about Australia, isn't there Senator?'

"What? Why do you ask?"

'Just curious. But they supported Uso Dex in the United Nations, and you're setting up that thing there for Dr Pink.'

"I like Australia, and I like Australians. Your mate, Nellie, there is a lot of the Australian in him. See if you recognize this person. He will take any amount of abuse from a mate, in public, but absolutely none from anyone else. He fears no one, crawls to no one, bludges off no one, and acknowledges no master. He says what he thinks. If he loses, a game, a fight, or an argument he laughs about it the next day. There is no one you would rather have beside you in a fight. And, if ever you are in trouble, real trouble, you'll find him standing right there beside you, no matter how badly you've stuffed up."

'Yeah, that sounds like Nellie.'

"That's how Australians were described by a bloke called Nino many years ago...."

'And you don't like New Ziland?'

"No. I do not like New Ziland. It can be a nasty little country. Hypocritical, smug, sucking up to the big countries. If New Ziland were a kid, it would be that slightly creepy one who is always hanging around, on the edges but never in. That kid you'd never let babysit your little sister, although you can't quite put your finger on why. The one who starts off pulling pony tails, and gets worse. New Ziland requires its people to conform, difference is sneered at, and the kid who rises above the others is pulled back down to size. An Aussie plays to win. A New Zilander is happy just to do better than his neighbor.

Many of the people we value most highly in Uso Dex have fought to retain their individuality in cultures which try very hard to turn out people like Big Macs, everyone the same. Most New Zilanders prefer the safety of the herd."

The Senator stooped speaking and looked at Sandy. "I'm sorry Sandy. These are just my views. I shouldn't be dumping them on you."

'No, go on. It's interesting.'

"Well, you saw that policeman shoot Adam yesterday. He was scared, a coward with a gun. But he will stay a member of the police. Our brother David was poisoned by his wife in Palmerston North. The wife said it was suicide. John Cleese, British comedian, once said "If you wish to kill yourself but lack the courage to, I think a visit to Palmerston North will do the trick." But our brother did not kill himself. He was a visiting professor at the local university. The first police on the scene thought his wife was acting - she was yelling but there were no tears. She 'just happened' to turn on her cell phone when the police were there and there was a suicide text from our brother. She produced a suicide note, but when we pointed out that the signature was not his, she produced a second, unsigned, suicide note. Despite the suspicions of the first policemen on the scene, the senior officer back at his desk, Dick Prosser, decided this was a suicide. It took four years to charge the wife with murder. Dick is now a member of parliament in New Ziland.

That's not the whole story Sandy. There are many excellent New Zilanders, people whom we would accept, and have accepted, as citizens, like Citizen Major Bolton. But more and more the good ones are becoming the exception. They are being driven from the cities to small towns like Cambridge."

'Is that why we won't help with this vaccine thing?'

"We are going to help. Red insists on it. He's been working night and day. First to develop an anti-toxin, and then to mass produce it. But our help will be provided secretly. We have provided the anti-toxin to our people in New Ziland. But no, one reason I don't care if New Ziland lives or dies, is because the world won't miss those people when they are gone. There is nothing special about New Zilanders. Americans, the English, the French, Italians, Australians, the Japanese, the Chinese, Xhosa. It's a long list of groupings that bring something to humanity. New Ziland has achieved its goal of fitting in, of not standing out, and it won't be missed. But, the main reason is that New Ziland is a country where a strong leader, a Nazi dictator, could come to power and could rule."

'So, why don't we, if we're going to war and all, why don't we let this thing kill the Alphas?'

"We could have killed the Alphas years ago, Sandy. We've had the biological weapons. But even a ninety per-cent kill rate would leave us outnumbered ten thousand to one. But there's a more important reason."

'Eh?'

"Alphas breed citizens. Not often, but among the billions of Alphas are hundreds of thousands of citizens we haven't identified yet. We want as many of them as possible."

Yep, that made sense. Jeez, this command business was tough. Mind you, at least Sandy had found out why there were Alphas.

Chapter Sixteen

Back on the reservation at last, and Corporal Afa wanted a chat.

"Founder, a word if you is having a moment?"

'Yep. Of course.'

"We is going to be very short of space in the house for a few days. It is being helpful if recruit Abel could share your room, at least until things is settling down."

'No problem, Corporal. I've never had a room of my own till a few nights ago. I'm used to sharing.'

Nellie, Jane, and Abel were waiting for him in the lounge.

"Yoo, boss boy, you got any plans? I got training soonish. But we better get Abel sorted before then. He got no clothes, no spare uniforms, no toothbrush even. And you gotta find us a ping pong table for after dinner. This fool reckons he can play. I gonna kill him."

'Everyone here is going to be pretty busy this arvo. We'll have to look after ourselves. How about we find a terminal and get Abel some gear ordered? There's one in my room.'

Down the hall, up the stairs, and into Sandy's room.

"Hey, you gotta big one Sandy. It's as big as our dorm."

'It's not as big as our dorm. Jane, can you work the computer? Better teach Abel too.'

"Any idea how we log-on here? There's no fingerprint port."

'Suppose we just use our school log in?'

Jane tried this. Alarms went off, in the house. "Intruder Alert. Commander's sleeping quarters. Intruder Alert."

A stern face appeared on the screen. "Identify yourself. You are in a restricted area. Stay where you are and await the arrival of security forces."

The bedroom door crashed open. It was Gunny, followed by Corporal Afa.

"Lieutenant, what have you done to alarm General Dean's internal security people?"

'We were trying to log-on to order Abel some gear and some clothes.'

"It's being OK, Citizen Master Gunnery Sergeant. I is handling this."

"Very good, Corporal. Carry on." At least Gunny was gone.

Corporal Afa approached the monitor.

"Alarms off. Identify yourself security officer."

That's weird, thought Sandy. His English is suddenly allgood.

"Security officer Delta2 Peter Symons, Citizen Corporal."

"Very good. I see you can read the information on your screen. Can you tell me who attempted to log-on to the system."

"Ahh, it was Citizen Jane, Corporal. But she used a school login and password."

"It was indeed Citizen Jane, security officer, and she can log in however she likes. Do you accept that?"

"Yes, Citizen Corporal."

"And has your system identified the people in the room with her when she logged on?"

"Citizen Nelson, a visitor, and…..a founder. I'm sorry Sir, I acted too quickly."

"There's no harm in that security officer. The visitor, he is Citizen Candidate Abel, a permanent resident yet to be chipped. ….Recruit Abel would you take off your uniform please? Leave your boxers on. But stand at least one meter from any wall or other person….Mr Symons would you record the biometric data for the citizen candidate please?"

"Certainly Citizen Corporal…Citizen Candidate, you will see a blinking light in the ceiling. Could you hold your right hand up to that please, fingers spread….The camera needs a good view of your fingertips. Thank you, now your left hand… Thank you. Arms by your side, would you look at the light please…Open your eyes wider if you could. Thank you. Scan is complete Citizen Corporal."

"Could you transfer all, on behalf of Founder Sandy, ordering and command privileges from Citizen Master Gunnery Sergeant Shane to Citizen Candidate Abel please?"

"I'm sorry Citizen Corporal, that requires authorization from either the Citizen Master Gunnery Sergeant or from Founder Sandy."

"Do you recognize the presence of Founder Sandy?"

"Founder Sandy is in the room with you Corporal."

"Founder, would you mind?"

'Yeah, whatever Corporal Afa asked for, do that please.'

"Certainly, Founder. How else can I be of service today?"

"The founder would like to order some personal effects for the citizen candidate and perhaps for others. He is not familiar with the system. Could you assist the citizen candidate?"

"Of course. Citizen Candidate, what personal effects are you looking for?"

"All of them. This is a borrowed set of boxers."

Corporal Afa motioned to Sandy, and they left the room.

"My apologies, Founder. I is not realizing you would think of doing these things for yourself. To be using any monitor on the reservation, just say 'HAL'. It is cutting out all the crap, and HAL is seeing you right. We is not normally dealing with the bureaucrats. If it is ever happening again, just be asking the system to confirm your identity. Be ignoring the human, or Choo. Then tell it what you is wanting. You is being a founder. You can be having everything."

'Ehh?'

"The system is giving you whatever you ask for, if we is having it on the reservation. You is being a founder. All other founders, including HAL, is being notified of every request you make, but none of them, except for HAL and maybe Citizen Administrator Luke is keeping up with all the data they is receiving."

'Thanks, CC. I better get back in there before Nellie clicks to this and tries to get Abel to order him some big guns and bombs.'

Corporal Afa gave Sandy a strange look. He didn't know Nellie.

Back in his room, it seemed that Abel had finished ordering.

"The goods will be delivered this afternoon, Citizen Candidate."

"Thank you."

"Hey, Sandy, you wanna swap beds?"

'Ehh?'

"Well, if you aint gonna sleep with Abel you need two beds. There's two beds in our room, but we only using one."

'Ehh?'

"And we could use a nice big bed like you got. She kicks real bad. And she steals the blankets. Not really sure it's worth it."

Nellie got a slap around the head for that. The penny dropped.

'Yeah, sure. But change the sheets you grub, or make sure Abel gets that bed.'

"Change the sheets."

Moving the beds was fun. Then they went looking for the laundry to get clean sheets. They had an eye out for a few chairs that needed liberating, and a coffee table for Sandy's room so they could meet in there.

They didn't get past the dining room. There were nice smells coming from the kitchen and Nellie decided he needed a snack before training.

Gunny was in the dining room, at a table with sergeants Max and Harley. Sandy went over. The two sergeants stood. That was embarrassing.

'Sit down, please. Gunny, there's a lot of work to do. Anything I can do to help?'

"Citizen Lieutenant, you are an officer. We try to keep officers as far away as we can from work. Involving them doubles the work, and triples the time it takes to complete it."

The sergeants nodded their agreement, vigorously.

"Anyway, I see that you are looking after yourself, and sorting the citizen candidate out. That is, actually, really very useful. Carry on."

Somehow conversations with Gunny just didn't work out the way Sandy thought they should. Oh well.

Back at their table Abel had had an idea. "Why don't we just ask the computer where the laundry is?"

'HAL? Don't you think he has more important things to do? Like save the reservation from imminent invasion? I'm not asking HAL the way to the laundry.'

They found a terminal. Abel spoke to it. The laundry was in the basement.

Nellie decided it was time for him to get ready for training. Sandy thought he would go the gym before dinner. Abel and Jane had another conversation with the computer, and decided they would go and pick up some ping pong gear and chairs and stuff from a warehouse. A van and driver would meet them outside in ten.

Sandy realized he had made a mistake sending Jane and Abel out together. It was fine when the clothes and stuff Abel had ordered from his room were delivered. Well, mostly fine. Sandy had been having a quick snooze after his workout and before dinner when there was a knock on his door.

Three troopers were there, each with their arms full of stuff.

That wasn't too bad. But Abel and Jane had left in a van. They came back in a truck. And Sandy didn't know the half of what they'd brought back. He got told to take the chairs and table up to his room. By the time he'd done that, there were three ping pong tables being set up in the lounge.

Jane had had an idea. Sandy didn't like it when Jane had an idea. They involved lots of work, by him and Nellie most of the time. Most of the time too, her ideas weren't that legal. Mind you, she'd had lots of ideas worse than this one. A 1RR ping pong championship. Three troops. Three tables. Then the champions of each troop to play off for the title.

It seemed everyone was keen on the idea.

There was nothing the matter with dinner. Three meats to choose from, potatoes, and vegetables. Sandy didn't see Citizen Master Gunnery Sergeant Shane, which was good. He didn't know what Gunny would think about a ping pong tournament.

The corporals were at dinner. Corporal Stan from Charlie troop was keen to play. The other two said they could get by without him.

There was a bit of an argument about the rules in the Bravo troop qualifiers. Marty, their soldier Gooch, couldn't hold the bat by the handle. It was too small. So he held it in the palm of his hand. Couldn't complain about that, but he wanted to use two bats. One in each hand.

No-one had a rule book. Sandy had to decide. He said everyone could have two bats if they wanted. Jane said they weren't bats they were paddles. Abel reckoned they were rackets, with a wooden blade and two rubber sheets, one for each side. No-one else cared. Two bats.

Then there was another argument. Marty hit the ball so hard it sometimes smashed. Did that mean he lost the point if the ball didn't hit the other side of the table? Did the other guy lose the point if he couldn't hit a smashed ball back to Marty?

Jeez, this command stuff was tough. Sandy decided that smashed ball meant replay the point.

Marty won the Bravo troop comp. Twenty-two smashed balls. Four crushed bats.

The Charlie troop comp came down to a battle between Harley and Stan. It was a good match, but Stan was just too quick. He seemed to be moving into position even before Harley hit the ball. Harley played the nice shots, but Stan played the last ones. Ugly things they were too, half the time.

But it was the game between Nellie and Abel that everybody watched. Nellie was good, real good, but Abel was something special. Where Nellie played away from the table, big booming shots, Abel crouched over the table, hitting the ball on the up, and using the whole of Nellie's side to make Nellie run. It didn't always work, but when it did it was great. A little shot just over the net, to one side. Nellie charging round the side of the table to get it. A big deep shot. Nellie rushing back and returning the ball, diving to reach it. A soft shot to mid table, bouncing twice before Nellie could get back to his feet. Final score 21-17.

Marty beat Stan pretty easily. Abel didn't have much trouble with Marty. Two bats were great, but Abel worked him out. The shot straight at Marty, so he had to move one way to hit the ball. Then the shot to the side Marty had come from. Gooch do not scramble well. 21-11, and Abel was 1RR ping pong champion.

"Did you see him? Eh, Sandy, did you see him? That Abbey, he can play. Killed me. I'm stuffed. Hey, let's get something to eat."

Chapter Seventeen

Oh five thirty. Sandy woke up. Damn, his body clock was back to normal. The shower was on. He looked across at Abel's bed, empty. A minute or so later Abel came out of the bathroom, still drying himself off.

"Good morning, Lieutenant. Into the shower with you now please. Your PT gear will be ready when you get out. Come on, chop-chop."

Sandy really thought that as he was the lieutenant, every now and then he should get to give the orders. But he got up, got into the shower, and another day started.

First, the run. Of course Nellie was waiting in the corridor, bouncing on his toes. Jane was stretching.

The run wasn't that simple. He had bodyguards now. A lead car in front and a chase car behind. Forty minutes. Quite a nice area to run in really. Twenty minutes out and then twenty minutes back.

Nellie had planned this. Sandy could tell. They went from the run to the shooting range under the house. Fired off some rounds. At least Sandy got to have a rifle, even if it was only for twenty minutes or so. Abel had never fired one before. It was five minutes before the range sergeant would even let him touch a weapon. But he got the hang of it pretty quickly. And they didn't have to clean their rifles. Cool. "But don't get used to it", the range sergeant said. They'd have their personal rifles issued later on in the day. Those would be cleaned after every time they were fired, and twice a day just for the fun of it. "Not you, Sir. I see you aren't to be issued with a rifle. Gunny's orders." He'd have to talk to Gunny about that. Tell him what was what. Deffo. Maybe later on. Yep, laters. Wonder if Gunny was ever in a good mood?

And then to the gym. Jane and Abel paired off for some one on one unarmed stuff, so did Nellie and Sandy. This was fun. Nellie was keen on Mixed Martial Arts. Sandy was a Muay Thai boy. Nellie was quick, and bigger. Excellent fun, sparring. Sandy just had to make sure Nellie got no chance for a takedown. On the ground Nellie's weight was a big advantage.

Showers back in their rooms. Into uniform, and down to breakfast at oh seven forty-five. Someone had given Abel one of those pesky tablet things.

"Lieutenant, I see you are down for a meeting at the Senator's place at oh nine hundred hours. Corporal Afa has left me a note to check that you can find your way there."

'Course I can, it's just next door.'

"Then this afternoon 1RR is to meet some visiting Australians. Oh, it's a television crew came to film the big game tomorrow. Hey, I know him. Tom Bishop. And Bill Silver, Bushie, he's coming too. And Dan Goldman from Maori television."

'What are you guys doing while I'm having my meeting?'

"It sounds like fun. We're getting personal weapons issued. Then joining the rest of the platoon for individual weapons training. You wouldn't like it. Grenades. Rocket launchers. Flame throwers. Stuff like that. Not officer stuff."

Sandy was feeling just a little on the grumpy side as he walked up to the Senator's door. He cheered up when he remembered the door had been blasted a couple of nights ago. Fixed now.

Once again the Senator opened the door for Sandy.

"Come in, come in. I was hoping we could have a few words."

They went into the dining room, but the Senator showed Sandy to a couple of comfy chairs by a coffee table in the corner.

"I wanted to talk to you about the television crew arriving on the plane this afternoon. This is another Dreamliner. They will have been treated well. But the real cargo is one hundred and twenty ILFS, Cylons, HAL is bringing over to send to the New World."

Sandy was surprised. It showed.

"It has been a bit of a secret. HAL has a manufacturing plant in Western Sydney. We own a few old mines there, and it has been really quite easy to set up a research laboratory focused on producing robots for use in mining. I haven't seen these ones. They are going to be HAL's design. I just hope it's not a whole hive of bumblebees. Nothing should go wrong. I understand that HAL will tell them when the television guys have left and they can get out of their crates.

Oh, by the way, I have a meeting with President Trump tomorrow night, twenty thirty in Washington. That should be interesting.

Anyway, that's it from me. I'll let you get back to your men. Should be a fun morning. Blowing some things up and burning other things down. I better call in on Red. He hasn't slept since we got back. That man is absolutely determined to ramp up anti-toxin production. Oh, one last thing. What do you think of the Gooch and the Choo?"

'They're allgood. Why?'

"Just keep an eye open for me, will you? The Choo seem to be becoming quite hostile to the Alphas. You have probably noticed the way they butcher the spoken language?"

'Yeah, I quite like it.'

"When they are under pressure, in combat for example, their language is fine. I think they butcher the language on purpose. And I was surprised by how angry Corporal Dave was in that interview. Anyway, enjoy the rest of your morning."

It was fun. Grenades were OK. Flamethrowers were excellent. But the rocket launchers were best. Easy as to use. You put it onto your shoulder, flicked up the sighting window, lined up the target, and pulled the trigger. Soldier-proof. Really good backflame too. And those old trucks and stuff they were aiming at in the fields. Sure made them bounce around.

Abel, Nellie and Sandy were still talking about it over lunch. Jane was really excited as well. This morning she'd flown a helicopter, a real helicopter, for the first time.

The afternoon sounded a bit flat in comparison. Jane was pretty good, she was back in a flight simulator. But Sandy had to go to the airport to meet the league commentators from Australia. So did Nellie. Both teams were to have afternoon tea with them. Abel was coming along too. It meant Sandy had to wear his number ones. Official like. Repping the unit. Nellie and the teams got to wear tracksuits.

She's a cruel thing sometimes, life.

Back to the airport. It was kinda fun sitting up front with the truck driver. Not so good that Abel was sitting beside him with his personal weapon, a rifle. Yep, Sandy thought, I'm really going to have to tell Gunny what's what about that. Deffo.

The television guys were allgood. Tom Bishop wasn't any bigger than Abel.

Old Bushie, Bill Silver, had been a player and a great coach, the most successful New South coach of all time.

Dan Goldman, from television in New Ziland was fine too. He came across for a chat with Sandy and Abel.

"So, I guess you two aren't in the team."

'Nah, we're not. Rugby league's not my game. Not big enough.'

"I've never played. My father wouldn't let me."

"You sound like a New Zilander. Where are you from?"

"Auckland. Only got here yesterday."

Dan gave Abel a long look. "Don't tell me. Are you the boy that escaped?"

"Yep, that's me. On the run. In the army now though."

"What do you think of it so far?"

"It's been cool. I've made friends with Nellie. He's a bit crazy, but allgood. Sandy's pretty good too. Mind you, I've got to say that. He's my boss, and he's standing right here next to me. And he rescued me."

"Was that you? The young chap in the excellent suit?"

'Yeah. That was me.'

"Well, small world, eh?"

'If you don't mind me asking, how come you guys are here?'

"I'm not really sure. Bushie got the call and decided he was coming over. He got hold of Tom. My bosses heard about it, and got me a place too. No idea what kind of game it's going to be."

'It's going to be a good one. We watch the NRL over here. It's about the only sport we do watch. The Gooch love it. We played it a lot at school.'

"Are you guys any good at the game?"

'I reckon we are. But we'll see what youse think tomorrow. What are you doing tonight?'

"We have been invited to watch the defenders' gym session. Then we're having dinner with them, before we catch up with your guys after the captain's run. Your captain, Max, didn't want us filming the captain's run. Anyway, I better dash. I see the Senator and General Dean are here."

After a while the teams left, taking the television guys with them.

HAL arrived. The Cylon ILFs started emerging from the rear of the plane.

"Oh what?" Sandy overheard the Senator. "They're exactly out of Battlestar Galactica."

"Yes, Senator. I thought about painting them in Bumblebee colors, but they're fine like this. We'll just pop along to the gate. I'll be gone for an hour or so."

They were. Cylon centurions, straight out of Battlestar Galactica. Dull silver in color. Two legs, two arms, a head, but quite clearly robots, not human.

Then they were gone. They were quick.

"Well, Gunny, that should speed up construction."

"Agreed, Senator. All the Gooch and Choo who are leaving are now on the other side. With the ILFs through too, all we are doing for the next twenty-six days is transporting goods and materials, and humans."

"And we have enough of those. We've been buying stuff up for the last twenty years. Pleased to get rid of it."

Chapter Eighteen

The captain's run. Something of a tradition. The boys go through their moves on the match field. Light work-out. Takes an hour or so. Then back for a feed and an early night.

This was Max's gig. He was the captain. Sandy thought he'd tag along. He didn't know many people and most of them were on the team. Jane was busy, having another session on the flight simulator. Abel was going. He wanted to be involved. Told Gunny he'd be water boy. Anything to be close to the action.

It finished up being pretty much a platoon deployment. Sandy was up front in the command vehicle, with one of the 1RR drivers and Abel. Abel had a rifle. Sandy didn't. That sucked.

The team followed behind in a troop carrier.

A second carrier containing a troop of sentries brought up the rear. Gunny sure took security seriously. He didn't care that they were still on the reservation. He wasn't going to rely on General Dean's men to provide security for his team. Especially not the day before the big game. So they were armed. Sandy had his pistol, and his knife. Abel had a rifle. Not fair that. Not fair at all.

Sandy reckoned Gunny wanted the team in war mode before the game. Cunning that. Gooch psychology.

And so here they were driving through the forest, heading towards the turbines. There were gates, and guards. The driver dealt with them.

Over to the far end of the landing area, and debus.

This time they jogged to the training area. Two of General Dean's men were doing guard duty at the beginning of the lake road. Sandy recognized Joshua Thomas, the loosie who had kneed Nellie in the school game. Nice uniform. He had a rifle. This was starting to irritate Sandy. He'd have words with Gunny about it.

Tell him what was up. Maybe after the game. Deffo after the game.

The warm up was boring. Sandy watched it for a while. But he wasn't a watcher. Thought he might wander down to the lake. Never been there. No point in jogging.

Now that was strange. The guards were gone. Maybe not. There was a group of them coming up from the lake. They weren't wearing the same uniform as Joshua Thomas had been. Hey, their rifles were different.

Sandy pulled his pistol from his belt holster. Safety off.

They spotted him. Two raised their rifles. Sandy dived towards a fissure in the rock and landed on Joshua Thomas. Dead Joshua Thomas. He stood up, pulling JT in front of him, poked his head around the corner and fired some shots at the oncoming invaders. Except they weren't there anymore. Sneaky buggars had taken cover. He heard firing and bullets smacked into Joshua Thomas.

The last thing Sandy heard was "Shots fired. Intruder Alert. Facility Lock Down. Intruder Alert. Shots fired." HAL was onto it. He's a good bloke is HAL.

Sandy woke up. He could hear rifle fire at the ground. He stood up. Dizzy. Sat down again. Stood up again. Picked up JT's rifle, and two spare magazines and started running towards the noise.

There were bad guys in front of him. Sandy could see four of them. Aim…fire. Aim…fire. Aim…fire. The fourth one had rolled into cover. Frig you. It's the friggin captain's run you moron! What do you think you're doing? Charge! Get out here where I can shoot your ass.

Sandy saw a rifle barrel poke up over top of the rock number four was hiding behind. He dived sideways and rolled, rolled again. There's the bad guy. Killed him dead. Good rifle.

What's that? Two more turning back towards him. One of them lifted his rifle to fire at Sandy. Dive, roll. Fire again. Missed. But now they are both hiding.

Sandy stood in the middle of the tunnel. JT's rifle swinging between the rocks behind which the invaders had taken cover. Pulled his pistol. Now he had two weapons and two rocks to cover. Allgood.

"Two drones now at your location, Lieutenant."

He's a top bloke is HAL. Sandy couldn't see the drones, but he heard the shots, and a body fell out from behind one rock. A blood trail started running from the other.

"Drones report that the passage is clear, Lieutenant. You may rejoin your unit. I have advised Gunny. Please stay in the middle of the path. Your men are jumpy."

Sandy holstered his pistol. He could see the field now, when he looked up.

"Sandy, fool", and Nellie was racing towards him, with Abel behind. "You stupid, stupid boy. What you doing going for a stroll like that? I can't leave you alone for a minute. You stupid, stupid boy." And Sandy was enveloped in a bear hug.

"Leave him alone Nellie. He's been shot. And look at all that blood."

"Shot? Where? Oh, in the head. Nah, that's the hardest part of him. Nothing to damage there. Look, the bullet bounced off. It's at the back anyway."

But Nellie did let him go. Both Nellies. Sandy did not feel well. He sat down again.

Now it was Gunny. Two gunnies.

"You two, carry him to the command building. Recruit Abel, I want that head wound cleaned and bandaged. Put pressure on it to stop the bleeding. Take his shirt off. Check for other wounds.

And where did he get that rifle? Jeez. Citizen Nellie, make that rifle safe. Both of you stay with him until he is back at our base. Do not let him out of your sight until I relieve you."

'Gunny, what happened?'

"We do not know Lieutenant. We were going through some kick return sets when the alarms went off. Seconds later four of our sentries were shot and killed. Corporal Afa has been severely wounded. He will be going back on the helicopter with you. We returned fire. HAL?"

"There has been an incursion into the reservation Master Gunnery Sergeant. Two teams of navy seals. Thanks to the lieutenant's warning the first team, the one that took the fork to the landing area did not make it to the command center lifts. The other six man team took the fork to your training area. Citizen Lieutenant Sandy killed four of them. He had the last two pinned behind rocks when the drones arrived and killed them.

General Dean is sending a full company to sweep the caves.

The med-evac helicopter is one minute out. Transport carts will be at your location in seconds."

Both Gunnys were looking at Sandy strangely. One Gunny was bad enough. Why did there have to be two of them?

Sandy did not remember much for a while after that.

CC Afa's groans, and a scream, as he was loaded onto the transport trolley, a golf cart really.

The wind, downdraft, from the helicopter as he was loaded onto it.

Vomiting in the helicopter. No idea where that came from. Abel wiping it up, and cleaning him off.

Worried snippets from the medics working on Afa. That sounded like Mr Bolton.

He turned his head to one side. He could see bubbles, blood bubbles, coming out of Afa's chest.

"Scalpel… swab here… chest drain… suture forceps… five oh silk.. Central line kit… Open the bag… Give him one liter Ringers stat…I need a chest theatre…prep for emergency thoracotomy on landing…no, on landing… I will open the chest on the way to theatre… what blood do we have on board?.. do we know this patient's type?… that's not going to do.. give him two units of human oh negative stat through the central line…… sister… I have a sucking chest wound…two other rounds in the chest, and two into the abdomen… suspected tamponade… I want an anesthetist on the landing pad… patient is intubated… I will proceed directly to open the chest… neurologically stable. I don't think we will need to open the cranium… If you have another surgeon available that would be helpful. There is a lot to do to save this chap…triage category expectant. I am instructed to save his life. He is a Choo."

Didn't sound good. Not good at all. Expectant. No, that wasn't good.

"Yes, there is a second patient. Vitals stable. Seems to have been shot in the head. Not penetrating. Triage category minimal. He is a founder."

Yep, Sandy thought, I sound pretty good.

The next thing Sandy heard was an argument. Nellie.

"Then we'll stay outside. Nah, I aint leaving my rifle behind. He's my mate and he just got shot right here on the reservation… Nah, we're staying here. He's not going anywhere without us right beside him…Who the frig are you… Major… Major pain in the ass… You aint the boss of me and if you aint gonna treat my mate, get your ass out of here before I shoot you."

And then Nellie again.

"He's asleep. What do you mean, is he in a coma? How should I know? I'm a shooter not a doctor. And I aint shot nothing yet. He got to shoot four people... You're TOM. I saw you on the monitor. You're supposed to be from outer space or somewhere."

Sandy opened his eyes. There was TOM, no, two TOMs.

'It's OK Nellie. TOM's allgood. He's a doctor.'

"Nah, you're not all there, in the head, Sandy. He's an alien. From outer space."

'Just get out of the way Nellie you FOB.'

"Hey, it said on the monitor that you're a robot. Mate, can I shoot you? Just a little bit, once or twice, for practice. I haven't shot anyone yet, and I'm getting behind. Sandy, he's shot four people, just today."

"Sandy, look at me please."

Yeah, TOM was a doctor. Sandy had to look at TOM's finger as he moved it round and about. He had to look at the light as it moved toward him and away. His knees, and behind his ankles, and the back of his elbows got tapped with this little hammer thing. It made his legs jerk and his calves and forearms twitch. And then TOM stitched up his head. "The bullet did a little more than just graze you Sandy. It's taken a chunk of bone out of the back of your skull, near the parieto-occipital junction. The dura is not exposed. I have applied some bone germinal matrix. You've got a concussion. That double vision and the vomiting, they were normal. Should go away in the next few hours. You can have something for the headache if you like."

Nah, it wasn't too bad.

"We're going to do an MRI scan of your head anyway, just to make sure there is no internal bleeding".

'How's Corporal Afa?'

"Not good. Mr Bolton is still operating. Been going for forty minutes now. It's an impossible job, but he's the best at what he does, which is battlefield trauma surgery. We've opened up a separate recovery ward for the platoon. There are a lot of folk up there. Let's get your scan done and you can join them."

"Hey Sandy man, he put polyfilla in your head."

The scan was weird. Lying flat and moving through this cylinder thing. The best part was when Nellie wouldn't leave his rifle outside. Nellie almost got himself choked to death as his rifle was pulled towards the machine, right up to the perspex shield, and the rifle strap was strangling him. That was cool.

TOM told Sandy he had a brain. Nellie reckoned that was a surprise, maybe it wasn't connected to anything? And there was no bleeding.

The hospital was full of soldiers. Nellie gave his rifle to one of the 1RR sentries, and the three of them went into the recovery room. They had to change into scrubs. All three troops of 1RR were there. So was the Senator. It looked pretty somber. As they walked through the door, everyone stood up and clapped.

Sandy had no idea what that was all about. It was no clearer when the Senator stood up and said,

"Captain, we are honored to have you here."

Sandy looked around. Who was the Senator talking to? There were a few laughs from the room.

"I'm talking to you Sandy. About the only bright spot from the evening is this video."

There were cameras everywhere. And the ones in the tunnels had captured all the action. There was Sandy wandering towards the fork. You could see the other guys coming up from the lake. Sandy draws his pistol. Some of them raise their rifles. You see Sandy dive into the gap in the rock. Bullets hit the stone around him. Then JT, dead JT is standing, well kneeling anyway, with

Sandy firing from behind him. JT is hit half a dozen times. Sandy takes one in the head and falls. You could see the bullet hit, and blood and tissue fly out.

The bad guys charge past. One of them stops at the gap and fires a couple of rounds into JT/Sandy. The bad guys move up, taking the path to the ground. Different cameras. They show the team training and the sentries watching the training, not the path. Gunny says something to Corporal Afa who runs over to the sentries.

CC Afa is hit, multiple times. It looks like he is dead. Four sentries are hit and killed.

The cameras switch back to Sandy. He staggers out of the gap in the rock. Blood is hosing from the back of his head, right side. Falls over. Gets up, sways. Takes JT's rifle and two ammo magazines. Then starts jogging unsteadily up the path towards the field.

The bad guys come into view. Sandy raises the rifle to his shoulder. He shoots while continuing to move forward. Three bad guys down. The fourth takes cover. Sandy does not take cover, He charges, dives, rolls, shoots. Four bad guys dead. Then the scene with Sandy in the middle of the path, pistol in one hand, rifle in the other, still bleeding, covering both rocks.

"Sandy, fool. You the man." That was Nellie.

"Citizen Master Gunnery Sergeant Shane Gooch insisted that you be promoted. He said he was not going to beat the lieutenant survival averages with you. Whatever that means." That was the Senator.

"Citizen Captain."

Oh no, here's Gunny. At least there is only one of him now.

"You may have a pistol AND a rifle, Sir. And you can keep your knife."

'Thanks, Gunny.'

"Hey, Sandy, look there's food." Nellie had spotted two tables.

Sandy found a chair and sat down. He was tired. And his head was sore. And Afa was getting operated on. And it was his fault. He wasn't sure how, but maybe if he had stayed with the men, his men, he would have noticed the sentries not paying attention, and they wouldn't have been caught by surprise. Abel sat beside him.

Nellie and Jane brought them over plates of food. Shane brought over a cup of hot chocolate. "It was a lucky day for 1RR when you joined us, Captain. And the evening is a good time to have hot chocolate."

At 02:32 by the clock on the wall, Mr Bolton came into the recovery room. He looked exhausted.

"I'm sorry. We did all we could, but there is brain damage. I don't think the corporal will be able to breath on his own for long. If any of you want to say goodbye, now is the time. Corporal Dave, I understand you were close. If you want to sit with him once we take the breathing tube out, for so long as it takes, you are welcome."

Sandy stood. 'I will sit with him too, if you have no objection Corporal.'

"We all will Mr Bolton. If you would extubate Corporal Afa and bring him here, we will do this together."

"Very good, Senator."

"HAL, could you arrange some mattresses and blankets please. We will sleep here tonight."

"As you wish, Senator."

Afa was wheeled into the recovery ward, on a hospital bed. There was a sheet over his lower body, but the bullet wounds, three in the chest and two in the abdomen were obvious, as were the two long midline surgical incisions, closed now with stitches. They ran from his neck to under the sheet, with a gap between them, perhaps as wide as a hand.

His breathing was ragged. It took him twenty minutes to die. The gaps between breaths got longer and longer, and then there was a last sigh. Sandy knew that Afa would not take another breath. He had felt something leave the body. He looked up. Others had noticed too. Dave, Nellie, Gunny.

For the whole twenty minutes, Corporal Dave held his friend's hand. Tears were running down Sandy's cheeks, had been for a while. Sandy could see a pulse in Afa's neck. His heart was still beating, although the breathing had stopped and life had left.

And then Corporal Dave was standing. He plunged fingers into two of the chest wounds, and when he withdrew them, they were bloody. He painted two lines of blood across his forehead.

"Afa, Corporal, you were my friend. I wear stripes of your blood, and I will avenge you."

Dave bloodied his fingers again. This time he leaned forward and painted the stripes on Sandy's forehead.

"Captain, thank you for killing those who killed my friend. I will follow you. O ta'engata pea ta'engata."

'O ta'engata pea ta'engata.' Where did Corporal Dave learn Tongan? Sandy didn't know much, but he knew that.

Nellie was next. As he was painted, "O ta'engata pea ta'engata". Then Abel. Everyone, even Gunny and the Senator were painted in Afa's blood. All of them repeated "O ta'engata pea ta'engata". Forever and ever.

General Dean turned up. He took Corporal Afa's dead hand. "I'm sorry Corporal. It was my job to keep you safe here at home."

The Senator came forward. "Thank you for coming Dean. Captain Sandy has already killed those who were to blame for the corporal's death. I only wish we could revive them so we could kill them again and again. We would all like a turn."

"I suppose we should call the game off now, Senator? It's hardly fair on your team."

"Nah. Get off. We're playing. Aren't we playing?"

"Yes, Citizen Recruit we are playing. Although we need a replacement loosie."

"I'll play Gunny. No probs." Abel?!

"Well, your team better get some sleep, Gunny. My men are up for this game."

"Thank you, Citizen General. But we will be playing for Corporal Afa. O ta'engata pea ta'engata."

Forever and ever. It sounded like a war cry, not a prayer the way Gunny said it. As soon as General Dean left, Gunny started packing the rugby league boys off to bed.

Citizen Sergeant Harley said he would sleep after the funeral. So did Citizen Sergeant Max, and Corporals Dave and Stan, the surviving Choo in the platoon. Shane wasn't sleeping yet. The Senator said he would stay too.

They shared stories about Afa.

Dave had a good one. Afa always reckoned that one of his ord ancestors had been a bank robber. When he was finally arrested and put in prison, they never found the money. Anyway, he's in jail and he gets a letter from his father. Son, it reads, it's time to plant the vegetable garden, but my arthritis is playing up. I'm not sure I can do it this year. Sure wish you were here. Well, the old fella gets a letter back real soon from his son. Dad, don't dig the vege patch. I've hidden the money there. The next day about a hundred police turn up. They dig and dig, but don't find any money. The old fella gets another letter. Dad, it should be allgood to plant the veges now. They read my mail here.

Harley told of a time when Afa put one over their Gooch sergeant, Mike. The one who had been killed in China. Afa was late to weapons training. He said he'd been helping move an elephant to the zoo. The poor animal had dropped dead in twelfth street. That wasn't why he was late. The official from the zoo, he had to record the death, but he couldn't spell twelfth. He couldn't spell eleventh either. So they'd had to drag the poor dead elephant over to tenth street. The ord could spell tenth.

That was funny. What was funnier was that there was no zoo on the reservation, no twelfth street, no eleventh street, no tenth street, and definitely no elephants.

More food appeared.

There were visitors.

Sandy didn't remember much about that.

"This game meant a lot to Afa. He wouldn't have missed it for the world. It's a shame he won't see it now."

"Dave, I think we can do something about that." The Senator stood, and put his hand on Afa's leg. He bent it. "We'll need to keep him cool. Is that OK by you?"

"Yes, sure. Whatever."

"In fact, we can do better than that." They talked for a while. Sandy was in a bit of a haze, but oh man, the Senator was a hell of a guy.

Chapter Nineteen.

"Are you sure, Senator, this looks like a very private time?"

The voice woke Sandy up. It was Bushie. Dave was still there, asleep in a chair, holding Afa's hand. There were new ice bags around Afa. They must have replaced them while he was dozing. The others were gone.

The Senator was at the door, with Bushie, Tom Bishop, Dan Goldman, and half a dozen other people, most with cameras.

"The team is still asleep behind the curtains. Just about time for them to wake up. If they don't want you here, you'll know about it."

Bushie walked up to Sandy. "It's an honor to meet you son. I'd have you on my team." He must have noticed Sandy's confused look. "We saw the video, and the hole in your head."

Sandy looked at the clock. 11:15.

"Get a shot of that flag."

That was one of the new guys, without a camera. Sandy looked around. It wasn't there before, but yeah it was O4 awesome. There, on the wall, was the new 1RR flag. 1RR in the top left. In the middle an embroidery of Sandy from the video, with rifle in one hand, pistol in the other, pointing at the two rocks. A body had fallen out from behind one. A blood trail led from the other. And wonderfully, it wasn't his picture. It was CC Afa, in camo pants, shirtless, bleeding from his five bullet wounds. And from below the 1RR, curving to the bottom right of the flag, around and under Corporal Afa, O ta'engata pea ta'engata.

There was a noise from behind the curtains. Gunny Shane, still in surgical scrubs, obviously he'd slept in them, pulled back one of the curtains. He saw the flag, stood to attention, thumping one foot on the ground as he did so, and saluted. One by one, the rest of the team came out from behind the curtains. Soon they were all there, in a line, at attention, saluting their flag and Afa. Half of them were in scrubs. The rest just in boxers.

"That will do, team. Out of here. Show us how, Corporal." And they were gone, following Corporal Stan out of the room.

"They are on their way back to their barracks to have breakfast and get into their training gear. Sorry, no cameras there. Not this morning. You won't see them again until they arrive at the ground."

"This is unbelievable." It was Dan Goldman, the commentator from New Ziland. "But how can they play today?"

Sandy was surprised to hear Tom Bishop. His voice sounded husky. "They can play. I hope they win."

He walked up to Sandy, and shook his hand. "Me too, I'm real proud to meet you, Sir."

Sandy was embarrassed. And then Dan Goldman came up. He was rescued by the Senator.

"We had better leave here. Gentlemen, we will take a helicopter to the area where the playing field is. You want to start broadcasting in half an hour. Sandy, you're with me please. We will have a clean uniform for you at the ground."

The big helicopter was waiting for them on the roof. So was General Dean. The three of them sat apart from the television guys. They were taken from the landing area to the ground in open carts. Armed soldiers were positioned every ten meters or so.

In the command center, Sandy changed into his clean uniform, captain's pips and all. It wasn't a fair trade – two pips for Afa.

Today there was a big screen on the far wall. The broadcast was just beginning. It was Dan Goldman.

"We didn't know they existed a few days ago. Now we hear that the only sport played by Gooch and Choo is rugby league and the main game of their season is an armed forces grudge match, between 1RR, a recon and rescue force, and the defenders, a reservation based force.

Here, it's midday Saturday. For our viewers back in Australia, New Ziland, and the Pacific Islands, it's early Sunday morning. I promise you, this is going to be a game worth staying up for, worth getting up for. If you've got mates or family still in bed, get them up. This is one game you are going to want to say you've seen.

I'm Dan Goldman, and with me in the commentary team today are two men who need no introduction. Bill Silver, the most successful Blues coach of all time." The screen showed Bushie, "And Tom Bishop who led Souths to their first championship in forty-three years, playing on after he suffered a broken cheekbone in the first tackle of the grand-final."

The screen showed that famous head clash, and shots of Tom during the game with the hollow in his cheek, and then the swelling clearly visible.

"Stay with us, for what must be the most dramatic pre-game in the history of rugby league, and for an act of heroism that defies belief."

And there's the clip of Sandy, covered in blood and bleeding from his head wound, staggering out of the gap in the rock. He falls over. Gets up, sways. Takes the rifle and two ammo magazines, then starts jogging unsteadily up the path towards the field.

"But now, let's meet the players. First the defenders. They had a gym session last night, before the game. Here's their captain, Sergeant Charles Gooch with Tom Bishop."

Charles Gooch is big, even for a Gooch. He comes up to Tom who is sparring with a punching bag. Tom moves aside, and Charles jabs the bag which explodes, covering them both in sand. The clip moves to a weight bench. Tom bench presses 140 kilos, about 300 pounds. Pretty good. Charles is at spotter. He curls the

140 kilos. Incredible. Then he signals off screen. A much thicker bar is brought over, and 50 kilo weights are loaded onto it. Ten of them. Five hundred kilos, eleven hundred pounds, plus the bar. Charles completes three sets of eight.

Tom Bishop has this to say. "And there are four of them on the defenders team. Props. Tonight, I'm happy to be retired."

The cameras spend another ten minutes with the defenders. Then it's back to Dan Goldman.

"1RR decided on a captain's run the night before the game. It's a bit of a mission to get to the field." A clip of the three vehicles making their way through the jungle, and coming up to the gates. Video of them jogging to the ground. Video of the warm up. Players setting up for the kick returns. A few of these. Gunny looks towards the sentries, says something to Corporal Afa who runs over to them. Shooting. Afa falls, as do four of the guards. Fire is returned by the other sentries. The team pepper pots to their weapons.

"This was not a drill. The reservation was attacked by a team of navy seals. Those four soldiers are dead. The Choo who was running towards them, Corporal Afa, is severely wounded. But what is happening down the tunnel, that's incredible."

And Sandy sees it again. There he was walking casually towards the fork. The other guys are coming up from the lake. Sandy draws his pistol. Some of them raise their rifles. Sandy dives into the gap in the rock. Bullets hit the stone around him. Then the dead soldier is being used as a shield, with Sandy firing from behind him. The shield soldier is hit half a dozen times. Sandy takes one in the head and falls. A replay in slow-mo of the bullet hit, and in slow-mo the blood and tissue fly out. Sandy was sure he could see bone chips flying.

The navy seals charge past. One of them stops at the gap and fires a couple of rounds into the dead soldier/Sandy. They take the path to the ground.

Sandy staggers out of the gap in the rock. Bleeding from his head. Lots of blood on his uniform. He falls over. Gets up, sways. Takes the dead soldier's rifle and two ammo magazines, then starts jogging unsteadily up the path towards the field.

The navy seals come into view. Sandy raises the rifle to his shoulder. He shoots while continuing to move forward. Three down. The fourth takes cover. Sandy does not take cover, He charges, dives, rolls, rolls again, shoots. Four navy seals dead. Then the scene with Sandy in the middle of the path, pistol in one hand, rifle in the other, covering both rocks. A dead body falls from behind one rock, blood flows from behind the other.

The clip continues.

It shows Nellie running up to Sandy. The whole 'you stupid boy' thing. Gunny's instructions to Nellie and Abel.

Sandy and Afa being loaded onto the helicopter. Mr Bolton desperately trying to keep Afa alive. His conversation with the medics and with the hospital.

Voiceover from Dan Goldman. "For those of you who don't know, expectant is the military triage category used to describe wounded soldiers who can't be saved given the resources available. These are the soldiers whose deaths are expected. Minimal means treatment can be delayed with no long term threat to life, limb, or sight. They're tough over here. Maori tough. If you survive getting shot in the head, that's minimal. You can wait in the queue for treatment."

Another clip, in slow-mo of the bullet hitting Sandy.

The helicopter landing, on the roof. Sandy hadn't seen this before. A nurse comes running with, well, a toolbox. Afa is placed on something with wheels that leaves him at chest height. Mr Bolton steps on a small platform and they, bed and platform are pushed towards a lift. Mr Bolton slashes a deep cut down Afa's chest. He is handed, what, a saw, and begins cutting, splitting the sternum. They are in the lift. "Chest retractor". He is handed something which he places in the wound and uses to separate both sides of the chest. Not another word has been spoken. The lift doors open. He is handed a scalpel. Oh man, that's Afa's heart. You can see it beating, in a sac thing. Mr Bolton cuts the sac, and blood pours out. That can't be good. A big swab comes into picture. Mr Bolton shakes his head. You can see his fingers in the blood, and he comes out with a bullet between his fingers. A dish appears, and the bullet goes into it. Now the swab. They are in the operating theatre. Mr Bolton is stitching up Afa's heart. That was unbelievable.

Dan Goldman again.

"The surgeon is Mr Ian Bolton. Three days ago he was operating in Auckland hospital. It is rumored that he operated on Mr Adam Gooch, in an airport hangar, after Mr Gooch was shot by New Ziland police. He was suspended from practice by the Medical Council of New Ziland yesterday. But viewers, that is how it is done. You will never see better emergency trauma surgery than that. Done on the run. If you've still got friends and family who aren't watching this, get them out of bed. You haven't seen anything yet. This was at eight pm last night, our time over here."

The Senator had been talking. Clever. Dan Goldman goes on.

"But there was another injured person on the helicopter. Let's not forget about him."

Sandy hadn't seen this either. They are on the roof. He is also on one of those elevated stretcher things on wheels. But there is a nurse in front of the lift. With a soldier, an officer. And Nellie is having words. This bit he had heard before, most of it anyway.

"They won't let us take the patient, Major."

"Soldiers, you can't come into the treatment areas. Leave your weapons here and take that lift to the ground floor where you can wait."

"Nah thanks. We got our orders, and he's our mate. He aint going nowhere without us."

"You are not going inside the hospital with weapons."

"Then we'll stay outside. Nah, I aint leaving my rifle behind. He's my mate and he just got shot right here on the reservation... Nah, we're staying here. He's not going anywhere without us right beside him...Who the frig are you... Major... Major pain in the ass... You aint the boss of me and if you aint gonna treat my mate, get your ass out of here before I shoot you."

The major moved forward. "Soldier I have given you an order. Put that weapon down." He took another step forward. Nellie raised his weapon, pointed it at the major. The click as he offed the safety catch was loud, real noticeable.

Then Abel was there. Between the major and Nellie.

"Major, I've had enough of you." One punch, and the major was knocked out. "That's the kind of fight I like Nellie. Two hits. I hit him. He hits the ground." Abel picked the major up, threw him over his soldier and walked toward the lift. The nurse was squawking into a microphone on her blouse "Security, security to the rooftop landing pad."

Abel pushed the lift button. The doors opened. He threw the major into a corner. Something broke. You could hear the crack. "Nurse, you better get in here. And we need a new major, eh. This one's broken."

The nurse scuttled into the lift and Abel walked back to Nellie.

"Whaddya do that for? I woulda shot him."

"Yeah, that's why."

There was the ding of a lift arriving. It was the Senator. Then the clip moved to Sandy being examined by TOM, and the squeezing of, well it wasn't really polyfilla was it, into the space where you could see bone was missing, then TOM sewing Sandy up. The scene of Nellie almost getting himself choked to death in the MRI room.

Dan Goldman again. "Two different preparations."

The next clip showed the defenders, enjoying dinner together, playing cards. All very relaxed.

Back to 1RR. Sandy entering the recovery suite with Nellie and Abel. Everybody clapping.

Dan Goldman again. "That was just about midnight here. Corporal Afa was still in surgery. The whole 1RR team is here, waiting for news. And then at half past two in the morning, this.."

There it is again. Mr Bolton coming in to deliver the bad news. The boys around Afa as he dies. The paintings. General Dean's visit.

Dan Goldman again. "And if any of you can watch that and still believe that these people should be shot on sight, may you rot in Hell. You probably think you haven't seen that young man with the head wound before tonight. He just joined the army here earlier in the week, with his two friends, Nellie and Abel, but if you live in New Ziland you have seen him before. He's this guy..."

This clip shows Sandy, in his suit, rescuing Abel, and their retreat, with Abel in a towel half running, half being carried between Sandy and Shane.

"He's the chap our prime minister has labeled a terrorist. And one of his mates is the young man he rescued, Abel, the son of Mr Adam Gooch. Abel who you have just seen deal to the troublesome major. Abel, who got stabbed twice in New Ziland two days ago, is playing today in place of Corporal Afa. It looks as though the prime minister has been pulling pony tails again...The teams will be arriving soon. We will shortly be going down to the locker rooms. The defenders are arriving at the ground now.. But

before we go, take a look at this. First, we have the defenders
.."

And the clip is of a team enjoying time together over breakfast.

"And then 1RR"

This is the clip of the team coming out from behind the curtains, and saluting Afa and the flag. You can see the mattresses behind them.

Now, it's Bushie speaking.

"Well, I've seen enough. Those two, Nellie and Abel are good enough for me. I've never seen them play, but I've got signed contracts here for them. The bad news is that Penrith is not the first choice for either of them. Nellie, he likes the Roosters. Abel is a Souths fan."

"Abel has never played the game before Bushie. His father wouldn't let him play in New Ziland. He tells me his son was too rough."

"That's good enough for me, Senator. What do you pay the lad? I'll double it."

"Oh, well Abel was on a soldier's pay, with danger money and allowances. But after last night, I've made him a citizen. That changes things."

"How much Senator? What's he on? I'll double it."

"He doesn't get paid as a citizen. So one dollar a year will do. But Souths have first option."

"Fair enough. I'll give them until kick off."

"Come on Russell. Get on the phone." That was Tom.

"And what about Nellie? I hope he's a citizen too."

"He is. That'll cost you another dollar."

"Unless the Chooks take him before kick-off."

Dan Goldman, again. "While we make our way down to the locker room to greet the defenders, have a look at this footage from our cameras in the locker room."

There is the sound of a phone ringing. A voice in the background says "It's for you, Mr Silver."

"Bushie here."

"Pay the man a dollar Bushie. Abel is a bunny now. Tom's opinion is good enough for me."

"That was quick. What do you think of it so far?"

"I'll do the movie for free. Just tell them to keep a part open."

The cameras cut to show the defenders getting off their carts and going into their locker room. General Dean is down there. It looks pretty professional as the players make their way to their seats, and are handed their jerseys by the general.

The camera cuts to Dan Goldman outside the locker room. "The defenders know nothing about last night, and we have agreed to keep the secret."

"Come on Sandy. Let's go downstairs. I want to see this." Sandy followed the Senator. They met the commentators outside the defenders' locker room.

"Is it OK if we have a look in your team's shed, Senator?'

"Sure Bushie, go right ahead."

Tom Bishop went in first. He came out pretty much straight away, tears visible on his cheeks.

"Crikey Senator, that's pretty powerful."

There was a muttered oath from the locker room. That was Bushie. The Senator went in, followed by Sandy.

Afa was there. Sitting beneath the number "13", wearing his jersey. Elbows on knees, chin resting on his knuckles. Hands closed into fists. Dead, but there.

It was Bushie, the super coach, who spoke. "Cripes Senator, you are some man manager."

Sandy and the Senator went outside. The 1RR team was arriving. They looked pretty flash in their training singlets.

"They'll warm up out here, and go inside thirty minutes before kick-off to get changed and rubbed down. Keep an eye out for Dave would you? He'll be coming into the locker room with us. You'll hand the players their jerseys, Captain."

The ground had filled up. The Senator said two thousand people could fit in around the field. It seemed pretty full already to Sandy. There was Dave. He jogged up to them.

"Come on you two. We should be inside before the team comes in."

The locker room was a big space. There were the seats. Behind them was the shower block. Nearer the door was an area with a couple of massage tables. For rub downs before the game, and medical treatment during it. Next to the showers was a large area with some gym equipment on the walls, and a big enough open area to throw a few passes. The commentators and cameras were in there.

Dave teared up when he saw Afa. "Thank you Senator. He was really looking forward to this game."

"He's part of the team Dave. O ta'engata pea ta'engata."

And then the team was filing in. Led by Citizen Sergeant Max, the captain. He started when he saw Afa. Stood in front of him, Struck himself over the heart with his right fist and boomed "o ta'engata pea ta'engata", parade ground voice, before taking his seat under the number eight on the wall. He was followed by Shane. Every player followed, striking himself over the heart and repeating "O ta'engata pea ta'engata", before taking his seat. Nellie, and only Nellie, stayed on his feet. Abel was the last to take his seat. When he was seated, Nellie took off his singlet, moved over to be in front of Afa and commenced a war dance, stamping, jumping, pointing. Sandy had never seen him do anything like this before. Abel recognized it, stood up, took his singlet off, and joined Nellie.

When they finished, and took their seats, they were pumped. Everyone was pumped. The Senator moved forward.

"The Sipi Tau, performed by the Tongan rugby team before a game. Men, there is not much for me to say. You know what today is about. It's not just a game of footie. It's the greatest day in any of our lives. Dying in your bed many years from now, you will remember today. You will remember how as young men you took this chance, this one chance, to tell our enemies, to tell the world, that they may take our lives but they cannot take our freedom. For we will fight, and continue to fight. And we will win. O ta'engata pea ta'engata."

The reply, from the seventeen seated players was thunderous. "O ta'engata pea ta'engata."

Ahh what, the Senator stole that speech from Braveheart!

Then it was all Sandy. He went up to Max, and gave him jersey number 8. The front of the jersey had been embroidered with their unit flag. Brilliant. There was Afa, pistol and rifle in hand, o ta'engata pea ta'engata.

Sandy didn't think Gooch could do it, but there were definitely tears there. He went around the locker room, and when all the jerseys were given out, he followed the Senator out the back door. They collected the television guys and went back upstairs.

Dan Goldman again. "So here we are folks. Set up for an incredible game. And that was an incredible privilege, being in the locker room for the giving out of the jerseys. I'd say those men were prepared to die for the Senator and each other. No doubt about it, but it's much more than that. However, being realistic the men of 1RR can't hope to win today, can they? I mean, one of their mates was killed last night in a terrorist attack by the United States. They've had hardly any sleep. It's obviously all pretty emotional. It's not possible to play eighty minutes of football on top of all that. What do you say, Tom."

"I don't know if I could do it. But these guys they are something special. I reckon we might see just how special in the next eighty minutes."

"And what about you Bushie?"

"I've had a bit of luck coaching in my time, and I've had some good boys to coach. But the Senator is something special. And so are the boys of 1RR. Regardless of the result today, I'm proud that Australia has taken the side of the reservation, and, I know I'm a little old for it, but give me a uniform and I'll stay here to defend the reservation against the United States. What about you two, are you in?"

"I'm in." Tom Bishop.

"It's only a game of footie Bushie. It's not worth shooting anyone over. Anyway, here come the teams onto the field."

1RR kicked off. The defender's captain, Charles Gooch got to make the first hit up. He charged up-field. Straight towards Shane. They collided on the twenty-meter line.

"What a collision. Two freight trains in a head on smash. And look at this, the first dust up of the game..."

The referee had called "held", and as the two players stepped back from one another, Shane had patted Charles on the cheek. Charles had responded with a solid punch to Shane's head.

"If that's your best punch, you're in trouble laddie." The referee was close enough that Shane's comment was heard by the commentators and the TV audience.

Then players were rushing in. General Dean grabbed the ground microphone.

"Sergeant Charles, stand down. Defenders stop right where you are. If any of you take another step forward, I'll come down and shoot you myself."

He had a great voice did General Dean. Order was restored before disorder had a chance to get underway.

The referee waved to the sideline.

"Would you look at that? I've never seen anything like it. That collision was so fierce they've popped the ball."

It wasn't long before 1RR was pinned in their red zone, defending that area between the goal line and the ten meter line. Four sets, twenty-four tackles, two repeat sets from penalties given away.

Of those twenty-four tackles, Abel was involved in half, either as tackler or second man in.

A chant went up around the ground "1RR, all day 1RR, all day." Dave was behind the goal line waving the unit flag.

Then a defender lost the ball in the tackle. It popped forward and was swooped on by Abel, who ran back behind the line. He yelled something to Nellie and booted the ball over the defenders, over halfway. It bounced and rolled to the twenty meter line, and Nellie was there. He scooped the ball up one handed and ran to dot down between the posts.

Bushie was out of his seat. "Brilliant play, and that boy has never played league before today. Stabbed on Wednesday. Water boy at training last night. Only got his jersey because there was no-one else when the number 13 was shot and killed. I love it. He's tackled his heart out, and when he got the chance he's turned the game around. That's the best dollar Russell will ever spend. And look at the winger, my boy. The Roosters didn't phone before kick-off. By crikey he's quick."

Easy conversion. Six-nil to 1RR. Twenty minutes gone.

Just on half-time they struck again. 1RR was enjoying a rare period on attack, twenty meters out from the try line. Stan got the ball, ran to the line and threw a long pass outside. It went to nobody, bounced, and was heading over the touchline.

Abel was there. He dived, and with most of his body in the air, out of the field of play, he caught the ball and flicked it infield, netball styles. Nellie caught it on the bounce. A Gooch to his right. He steps that way, then left. The Gooch is unbalanced and Nellie slides under his arm to score. Try not converted. Ten-nil at half time.

Bushie is out of his seat again. "Let's replay that catch and pass. All day. You'll never see anything better. It's individual brilliance that's breaking this arm wrestle, and young Abel is the go-to man for that."

The second half begins badly for 1RR. Sergeant Harley is knocked out by a late swinging forearm. Not seen by the referee.

The defenders have all four of their Gooch on the field. That's too much power in the middle. They score. 10-6

They try the same thing again. 1RR holds them out. Then Shane has the ball. He is held up in the tackle. Nellie runs in for the short ball. Shane gives it, and there's Nellie, two Gooch in front of him. Steps, steps, and runs between them. Only the fullback to beat. Easy. Eighty meter try under the posts. Converted. 16-6.

"He doesn't need much room that boy. He'll sleep in the crack under your door. And that step, step you right out of your boxers he will." Bushie had a way with words, especially when he was excited.

And then it happened. Nellie had come back into the middle to help out on defense. He was second man in the tackle, rolled away to clear the tackle area, and was on his back when one of the defenders ran up, kneed him, and punched him flush in the face. A sickening blow. Nellie lay motionless.

Shane and Max rushed up and stood over Nellie. It looked like being the brawl to end all brawls. Abel went for the guy who had punched Nellie. Knocked him out. Then he was surrounded by defenders. Punching, punching, punching. But Abel was going strong in the middle of it all. On fire.

Sandy got a fright. General Dean had jumped past him. He ran through the plate glass window onto the deck, glass everywhere, pulled out his pistol, and fired off a full magazine, nine shots in the air.

The players stopped, and looked up. The general was furious. "You, Enoka, when you wake up, COME HERE LADDIE! You're out of this game, and cleaning toilets for the next month. The rest of you, play footie. You're getting beaten. Harden up."

An excellent parade ground voice. Easily heard all over the field without any need for a public address system.

"Well, you don't see that every day in Sydney. An owner smashing his way through the front of his box and pulling a gun on his team." Dan Goldman.

"What a game. What a great game. But how's the lad?" Bushie was focused.

Sandy could hear through the referee's microphone.

"Whaddya mean I'm knocked out. I'm talking to ya aint I? Tell ya what, if I was dreaming it wouldn't be about you. Just winded that's all. Get out of my face and I'll be up."

Nellie was good to go.

But it seemed like the general's pep talk had worked. Or maybe the boys were just too tired. Two converted tries to the defenders. 16-18 with one minute to go, and 1RR back defending their goal-line.

"It's been a brave effort by 1RR, but just a bridge too far after the night they had. What do you think Bushie?"

"She's an eighty minute game Dan. It's not over till it's over."

1RR was squeezed in their right hand corner. The ball came back to Abel from dummy half. What was he thinking? An overhead pass, a gridiron pass, to the other side of the field. To Nellie. Who caught the ball and was off. Oh yeah, what a try. One hundred meters. Three players racing across. No way they could catch him. But he had the wobbles. Twenty meters from the goal line he fell, rolled, regained his feet, and was over in the corner.

A win, a fantastic win.

It wasn't until they were back in the locker room that Sandy realized the boys were all still painted. He was painted. The Senator was painted. But the day wasn't over yet. They still had to bury Afa. He had left the building.

Someone had brought uniforms. There were clean number ones on the hooks beneath the player numbers. And towels. The boys were buggered. Absolutely. Nothing left in the tank. They were chivvied into the ice baths. And then to the showers.

General Dean and Charles came into the room. They went round shaking hands. Charles asked if they could come to the funeral. "Yeah, but you leave that cowardly piece of dog crap Enoka at home, you hear." It didn't sound as though Sergeant Max believed that what happened on the field stayed on the field, not always.

The commentators wanted a word with Nellie, four try Nellie, but the Senator said no. "Just listen. That boy talks. You'll get your sound-bytes."

They did. Abel came up and asked Nellie how he was doing.

"I'm allgoods man. What was up with that last pass?"

"Eh?"

"Why did you throw two balls at me? Lucky I caught one of them."

"Why did you fall over before the try line?"

"Dunno. Must have been an earthquake or something. Did you feel it where you were?"

They had even brought a new uniform for Sandy. A suit for the Senator.

"I'm on a bit of a tight schedule. I have to meet President Trump at twenty thirty. I will have to leave straight from the funeral. You better get that dressing changed."

Sandy didn't think he needed to do that. Took the bandage off when he had a shower, and left it in a rubbish bin.

The trip back to the house was quiet. Afa was going to be buried in the front yard, with the four sentries. No cameras. Sandy didn't mind if the commentators attended.

Four coffins, and Afa wrapped in a white sheet. With a 1RR flag folded on his chest. The Last Post playing as he was lowered into the ground.

Sandy wanted the war to start. It was time for an extinction event, an Alpha extinction event.

Chapter Twenty

Sandy was just too tired. Nigh-nigh time, and it was only twenty hundred hours. Mind you, he hadn't slept much since oh five thirty yesterday. Just those naps at the hospital. Twenty-four hours ago he'd been stitched up and had the brain scan. Since then Corporal Afa had died, there'd been the league game (four tries to Nellie), and Corporal Afa had been buried. Nellie reckoned Sandy was tired because he'd been shot in the head, but what did Nellie know?

He thought about all this in the shower. Didn't get very far. Yep, it had been a long day.

Yep, bedtime.

He was woken up by Nellie diving on him.

"Cmon boy, whaddyathinkyourdoing? Time for brekkie."

'Gerroff me. I'm sleeping.'

"Nah, you're in the army now, Captain. We get up at oh eight hundred Sunday."

'What? Who made up that rule?'

"I did. C'mon. I'm hungry and Jane won't go to breakfast without you. She's been up for hours, she says. There's a war on, and we're missing out. China. And Mexico has invaded California and Texas. China bombed Pearl Harbor and Las Vegas. And someone bombed the Senator. He's dead. So's President Trump. No surprise. He was pretty old. I saw him the other day. Looked about ready to snuff it. China reckoned the Senator was his brother and declared war on America. Hurry up and get up. There's bullets flying all over the place and none of thems my bullets."

'OK, I'm getting up.' The Senator was dead? Last Sandy had heard he was on his way to a meeting with President Trump. Something must have gone wrong. Maybe not. Radio Nellie was good listening, but the news service was pretty unreliable. Jane would know.

Nellie got off him and started poking Abel.

"Abbey, hey Abbey, you dead or something? I just remembered that surgeon fella said it would take ten days for you to heal. You shouldn't have played yesterday. You were useless anyway."

Abel groaned, rolled over, and groaned again. He sat up, and Sandy saw his body was covered in bruises.

"I feel like I've been run over by a bus."

"Nah, worse. Gooch. Lots of Gooch. Lots of times. Get in the shower. Hot water is good for bruises. Had a few meself in my time. Twenty minutes in the shower and they feel much better."

Nellie went and had a look in the bathroom.

"Come on youse. There's two shower things in here. You can both shower at the same time. Hurry up. The war'll be over the rate you're going. And I'm starving. Now I know what those Africans feel like."

Sandy gave in, got up and into the shower. He was finished before Abel had got out of bed and dragged himself to the bathroom. Yep, there was a clean uniform in the closet.

'Go on Nellie. Go get a uniform on. You can't be in a war if you're not wearing a uniform.'

"Jeez, you could be right. Be a first. Back in a minute."

Sandy lay back on his bed, towel around his waist. Maybe he could hit the snooze button and grab five more minutes. No, it wouldn't work. Nellie would come bouncing back in. No point arguing with him. No way he was going to listen. He was just a big two hundred and ten pound puppy, and Sandy was going down to breakfast with him. Like it or not.

Sandy gave in and started getting dressed. He heard the shower turn off, and a minute or so later Abel came back in the room.

'You look like crap, mate.'

"Nah, it's much better now I'm walking around. I'm good to go. You found your uniform, all by yourself. I wasn't sure you'd be able to."

'Cumon, it wasn't that hard.'

"Yeah, but you're an officer. The corporals and sergeants seem to think that officers need a lot of looking after."

'I've only been an officer for a week, not even that. Maybe I'm still learning to be totally useless.'

"Maybe." But Abel sounded doubtful.

"Nah. He's always needed looking after. It's worse than ever now. He gets shot most every time I let him out of my sight." Nellie was back. That was hardly fair. He'd only been shot twice. Well, five times, but only twice really. Monday and the other day.

Breakfast was good. They were showing a replay of the game in the dining room. Most of the team was there. Even Sergeant Harley who'd been knocked out.

"I've got to watch this. If I don't remember the game when I see the doctor tomorrow morning I'll be stood down for two weeks – off combat duties."

'Will that fool her?'

"Not by itself. But we have to do concussion testing start of the year. Everyone tries to do badly then, so when we get tested after a knock, we compare pretty well."

"Shhush sarge. The walls have ears," and a kind of nod at Sandy. Paul, from Bravo troop, played left center yesterday, inside Nellie.

"What you saying fool? You don't trust my mate?"

"Nah, it's not that Nellie. But there's stuff you keep in the team. And officers, they hear things, they got to act on them."

"Leave it Trooper. The captain's a dude. He saved all our lives Friday night. If he wants to stand me down from combat duties, I'm stood down. No argument from me. Now how about you just shut up and watch the game."

It was a good game to watch. Nellie joined in the laughter, the congratulations for good hits, and the joking about misses and bump offs.

On the replay screen Nellie was getting knocked out, again.

"That Enoka. Time he got a hiding I reckon. He'll keep."

Good on yah Nellie. Get things into perspective.

And then the commentary team was there. No cameras.

It was Tom Bishop who spoke. "Hey, do you guys mind if we hang here for a while? It doesn't look like our flight is leaving today, with the war and all, and, well, winners are grinners you know, so it should be more fun over here."

Everybody looked at Sandy.

'Sure. The kitchen's through there. Grab yourselves something to eat. The boys are talking about the game. If you listen to them we scored about a hundred tries and made a thousand tackles.'

This command stuff got easier every time.

Bushie laughed.

It was comfy in the dining area. Lots of buzz. Laughs. Food. Warm.

Dan Goldman came and sat at his table. "A penny for your thoughts, Captain."

'You'd be wasting your money, Dan. I'm not big on thinking.'

"If you don't mind me asking, how old are you, Captain?"

'Seventeen. Just turned seventeen on Monday.'

"Isn't that awfully young to be an army captain?"

'I don't know. I've never met any other captains.'

"So what's your role in all this?"

'My team has to go fetch our citizens and employees who need extraction, from anywhere in the world.'

"Including New Ziland?"

'Yep.'

"What do you think of them, the Gooch and the Choo? I mean, you guys have turned the world upside down for them."

'Them. What do you mean them? It's we, the Gooch, the Choo, the Betas like me, the ILFs, and the Alphas who support us.'

"But you, you're like us. They're not. They look like us but they're animals with human genes added."

'I don't know about that. I reckon you're saying there's a difference. I don't see it. Your lot, they want to kill us. That's the difference.'

"But you, you're human."

'What's so special about being human? Anyway, it depends what you mean by human, doesn't it? Look at Abel. His dad's a Gooch. His mum is human. What's he? He's got gorilla and chimpanzee genes that no human has had for millions of years. He's got other genes that no human has ever had. I'm not going to let you kill him.'

"But, maybe if all the Gooch, and the Choo, and the half-breeds like Abel agreed not to have children, maybe we could let them live?"

'You just don't get it do you? It's not your choice. You guys are just about to start a world war. And there's that biological weapon out there. One of you will work out how to make it kill everyone. We develop an anti-toxin. You develop a weapon. You've got problems, much bigger problems than us. You're looking at the destruction of humanity but all you see is us. Get real.'

Sandy got up, and went to join Nellie and Abel.

Yeah, this was fun. Lots of food. Plenty of juice. Just like any other Sunday. Sitting round with a group of mates who were talking crap. The topic was still yesterday's game.

But it wasn't quite the same. Nellie, Jane, Abel, they were comfortable round him. But most of the others, it was like they were, well not scared, but a bit nervous to come close. He was getting lots of glances, but that was it.

Tom Bishop came up to him.

"For a young man, you sure have earned a big rep quickly, Sandy."

'Eh? What?'

"Well, look at these guys. They've got huge respect for you. You're up there somewhere, and they're not worthy. Hey, don't get me wrong. I'm with them. You're some kind of superhero to them, to me, and to a hell of a lot of people now."

'Well, I didn't mean to be.'

"Yeah, and that's pretty much the whole point isn't it? But what I really came over for was to tell you that they're trying to set up some kind of interview with you about Abel."

'Eh?'

"It's not really my business. But there's been a lot of TV coverage about Abel in New Ziland since he escaped. They're saying he killed some kids when he was about nine. TV in New Ziland wants to interview people here by video link. It's going to be your call. Apparently you are incredibly senior here. Much, much more than a captain. You never told us about that?"

'Well, nah, no reason to.'

Then TOM was there.

"Morning Sandy. I hear Tom has already spoken to you about this. Perhaps the interview might be useful."

'Why's that?'

"Well, you have some decisions to make about New Ziland. We have the anti-toxin. They have the illness and it's spreading fast. Over one thousand dead and five thousand cases. Their prime minister has asked for anti-toxin. It's big news over there now. Red wants to give them the anti-toxin, but he hasn't got any planes. You have. This interview might help you see the New Ziland point of view better."

'Yeah, but the boys are having a good time. I don't want to spoil their buzz.'

"If this interview goes the way I think it will, they will be on a new buzz. This will be a long party. What do you say?"

'OK. I'll have a word to Abel.'

"No. I'll handle that. I'll set things up."

Well, that wasn't much good. Sandy had something else to worry about and he didn't even know what it was. Not really.

And now it was Bushie coming up to him.

"Sandy, I heard about what is planned. With the TV, and the interview by that dickhead Peter Henley. I have been asked for my views. If you don't mind, I will give them."

'Yeah, sure. There's TOM over there. He's organizing it.'

It took a little while. TOM set up a big screen at the end of the room, and cameras. Cameras all over the place. Shane and Max turned up.

"Captain, are you sure about this?"

'Dunno, Gunny. TOM thinks it is a good idea.'

"No Gooch will ever argue with TOM. We will stay."

And then it was time. TOM stood in front of the big screen.

"Gentlemen, settle down and listen to me for a moment please."

Surprisingly, that worked.

"Captain Sandy has given permission for an interview by a television station in New Ziland. They are responding to something they have heard about Citizen Abel. Let me show you the video."

Sandy moved over to stand with Abel. Nellie and Jane were already there. Shane and Max moved over too. There was hardly room for Bushie and Tom Bishop. Another table was joined to theirs. Now there was room. Dan Goldman joined them.

On the big screen, there were two ladies being interviewed by some bloke, Peter Henley. They were talking about how their sons had gone to school one day. They were nine years old and had made fun of a big, clumsy boy in their class, Abel, and he had killed both of them. He was never charged. No-one had ever been held accountable for their sons' deaths. Now Abel had escaped from jail after being accused of serious drug offences, and he was being treated as some sort of hero after the league game, looking forward to a professional career while their sons were buried and would never have these opportunities. They didn't think Abel should have things that their sons could never have. Abel was an animal. He should be in a zoo.

Peter Henley was on the screen.

"We have asked the question of Souths. No reply from them yet. Now we cross live to the reservation, where we can ask the question directly of Uso Dex. Is Abel the kind of savage they are protecting over there? He is half Gooch."

Oh, this was HAL on the big screen, interrupting. He was in the war room, well the Senator's dining room, but it still looked like a war room. The monitors showed maps, with arrows, and there were live feeds. The Senator was there. So much for Radio Nellie news. Headlines were running across the bottom of a big screen monitor in the background "China declares war with cyberattack immobilizing US military...President Trump killed in nuclear strike on Washington DC...nuclear attacks on Pearl Harbor and Las Vegas...Mexico invades California... San Diego falls...President surrenders...mutiny by the joint chiefs...Texas invades Mexico... China takes Guam, invades Japan". Yep, the war was on. Excellent.

"Peter, you have not been particularly honest with your viewers. I have the police reports from six years ago. First, though let me show you the other boys involved." Nineteen pictures followed. Each of a fifteen or sixteen year old. HAL read out the details. Names, addresses, schools.

"Each of those boys was interviewed by the police. Those interviews are being transmitted to you now. They all agreed that the group of them, led by the two boys who were killed, had formed a circle around Abel in the changing rooms and were teasing him about his feet. He has splayed toes. They wouldn't let him go. Four of the boys held Abel and the two who were killed started hitting him. Abel lost his temper. Shrugged his shoulders, freed his arms, and hit those two boys back. Hard. The pathology report shows that one of them was hit twice in the head. He had two brain bleeds. The second was hit once in the stomach. He had a ruptured spleen. The nineteen other boys ran off. Abel finished getting changed. It was Abel who found a teacher and told him he'd been in a fight. It was another twenty minutes before the school called an ambulance. Another forty minutes before the ambulance arrived. By that time neither boy was salvageable."

Peter Henley again. "Even at age eight or nine, Abel was much bigger than the other boys. He was twice their size. This was a cowardly attack in response to a bit of schoolboy teasing. The sort of harmless teasing that happens every day in schools around the country."

Sandy looked at Abel. He had his head in his hands looking down at the table. Shane stood up.

"I am Citizen Master Gunnery Shane Cooch. Citizen Abel is a member of my troop. This news surprises me, and I am disappointed with Citizen Abel."

What? Sandy looked at Shane. The room was suddenly very quiet indeed.

"He only killed two of the offenders. All should die. Now the rest of us must tidy up after him. It is not good to leave live enemies behind you. HAL knows where they live, and where they go to school. The next time we are in New Ziland, I shall make the time to find and kill at least a few of them."

There were cheers in the room. "Leave some for me, Gunny", "Don't forget about me." Abel looked up.

Peter Henley. "Maybe we can't expect anything more from a trained killer monkey. But you, Nellie, you're human. Surely you don't condone what Abel did?"

Nellie stood. "Abbey's me mate. Who the frig are you?"

And now it was Bushie. "I don't think Peter Henley has a clue what you are on about Nellie. But let me show you something about this young man you are calling a coward. Remember, he's fifteen years old."

On the big screen there was the video of Sandy and Abel asleep. Cameras were everywhere on the reservation, and they were always on. Then in comes Nellie, diving on Sandy. Then the bit where Abel sits up. He looks a mess. Then Abel walking to the showers. He is a mess. Covered in bruises, shuffling.

"And this is how he got like that."

Clips from the game. Of Abel making tackle after tackle after tackle. Most of them on big angry Gooch.

"Peter Henley, you have never played a game of rugby league in your life. But I can tell you one thing. No one who takes the rugby league field is a coward."

There was banging on the tables. The team was pretty vocal now. "Good on ya Abel", "Well done mate", "All day, All day."

Peter Henley, again. "What about you, Captain? No one doubts your courage. Do you really think the strong should be able to do as they like to the weak?"

Sandy was angry. Really quite angry. This dickhead and the country that gave him television time could burn in hell. 'We have the anti-toxin you need. Yesterday, I would have delivered it to you. Not now. If you want it, you come and get it. I mean you, Peter Henley. You come here and I will fight you for it. Just you and me. You're bigger. No weapons. No matter who wins, you go back to New Ziland with an airplane full of anti-toxin. If you lose you go back in a coffin. Have you got the balls for it or are you the real coward here?'

The boys loved it. There was thumping on the tables. The chant of "Sandy, Sandy, Sandy.." started in the IRR dining room but the cameras showed it being taken up by soldiers all over the reservation. TOM was right. This was going to be a good party. Sandy looked over at his friends. There were tears running down Abel's cheeks. Nellie and Jane were chanting. Shane and Max both saluted him, then extended their hands to shake his.

The last word was with Bushie. "One thing I've noticed over the years. There be lions. I'm always surprised when someone tries to kick a sleeping lion in the balls and then starts crying foul when the lion wakes up. New Ziland, it hasn't always been a pleasure, but I will miss you."

Acknowledgements

If this book contains anything that is funny, or any dialog that is interesting, those passages have probably been lifted straight from conversations involving members of *Tamaki Sports Academy*. Those boys are not great readers, so I will more than likely get away with the various expropriations. The stealing was done fair and square in any case.

The members of the Ilkley Grammar School Book Club in West Yorkshire were kind enough to read the penultimate draft of *Citizen Sandy*. The book would be even worse without their feedback. My thanks are extended to Mr Sam Lord and to (in no particular order) Molly H, Tom B, Dan W, Emma S, Eloise H, Maddie F, Rosie M, Evie S, Matilda T, Bea R, Freya R, Francesca B, Izzy G, Imogen B, Josh B, Lucy H-R, Alice R, Marcus W, George L, Brody G.

Rhys Cullen, July 2016